# LOST IN THE WAR

## NANCY ANTLE

**Dial Books for Young Readers**
*New York*

Published by Dial Books for Young Readers
A member of Penguin Putnam Inc.
375 Hudson Street • New York, New York 10014

Copyright © 1998 by Nancy Antle
All rights reserved
Designed by Pamela Darcy
Printed in the U.S.A. on acid-free paper
First Edition
1 3 5 7 9 10 8 6 4 2

Library of Congress Cataloging in Publication Data
Antle, Nancy.
Lost in the war/Nancy Antle.—1st ed.
p. cm.
Summary: Twelve-year-old Lisa Grey struggles to cope
with a mother whose traumatic experiences as a nurse
in Vietnam during the war are still haunting her.
ISBN 0-8037-2299-0 (trade)
1. Vietnamese Conflict, 1961–1975—Juvenile fiction.
[1.Vietnamese Conflict, 1961–1975—Fiction.
2. Schools—Fiction. 3. Depression, Mental—Fiction.]
I. Title.    PZ7.A6294Lo    1998
[Fic]—DC21    97-18234    CIP    AC

*For Linda Gerner, sister and
friend, with love*

**May 1982**

*New Haven, Connecticut*

One

Sometime that night I woke up standing beside my bed. It took me only a couple of seconds to realize why. Thunder and lightning were exploding overhead. Hail was pelting the windows. I had jumped out of bed before I was even awake. Across the hall my younger sister, Jenny, slept on peacefully.

I knew right away what kind of night Mom would have. Aunt Rose had warned me. So had Dr. Haas. I hadn't known about the problems with storms until recently. Aunt Rose said that Jenny and I were old enough to know all about Mom now. I wasn't sure about Jenny—she's only eleven, but I'm almost a teenager and I guess that's old enough. Still, I wished Aunt Rose wasn't out of town.

"Mom!" I called. My voice was drowned out by an explosion of thunder.

Without thinking, I grabbed Dad's dog tag from my nightstand and slipped the chain over my head before I ran down the hall. The familiar metal tapped against my skin under my T-shirt, but it didn't make me feel better.

The lightning lit up Mom's room. The covers on her bed were rumpled, but she wasn't there. I felt a wave of panic. Then I heard a sound—a whimper.

I knelt beside the bed and looked under it. There was Mom, her pillow wrapped around her head. I touched her arm. She pulled back.

"Mom!" I yelled. "It's just a storm. It's okay."

She moved the pillow and reached out for my hand.

"Lisa?" Her voice sounded small and far away.

"It's just thunder," I said. She'd never told us about her nightmares—but I knew about rocket attacks from reading the journal she'd kept as a nurse in Vietnam during the war there.

She crawled out and sat on the edge of the bed. Her hands shook as she pushed her long dark hair back from her face. Her whole body trembled when the thunder crashed again.

"I can't believe I did that," she muttered.

I put my arm around her shoulders. I wasn't sure

what else to do. Aunt Rose lived with us on the third floor of our house. When Mom had trouble sleeping or had a bad dream, Aunt Rose would come down to talk to her. But Aunt Rose was away on a photo shoot in Mexico.

A year ago my aunt finally talked Mom into seeing a psychiatrist. Now that she was trying to remember everything about her time in Vietnam, it seemed like the nightmares were worse.

I had believed Aunt Rose when she said a psychiatrist would help Mom face her past and learn to live with it. I believed Aunt Rose when she said it would help Mom get over her depression. That night, though, I didn't know what to believe.

Jenny knew what to believe. She always had definite opinions about everything. She didn't like Mom remembering. But what did she expect her to do? Did she want Mom to cut a part of her brain out— the part that remembered her life in Vietnam in 1968—and box it up with all the other memories she kept at the top of her closet? Mom had tried to bury the past. It hadn't worked. For the ten years she had worked at Yale-New Haven Hospital no one had known she had served in Vietnam. She never talked about it.

Jenny liked it that way. She thought that remembering was what had made Mom depressed to begin with. She didn't want Mom to see a psychiatrist and remember even more.

"All it will do is make her sadder," Jenny had said.

But even Jenny had to admit that Mom couldn't forget Vietnam because she couldn't forget Dad. There's always Jenny and me to remind her. We have the same blue eyes and blonde hair that Dad had. Jenny has his smile. So sooner or later Mom starts thinking about Dad, which of course makes her think about Vietnam since that's where they met. And where Dad died.

Dad's picture stared at me from beside the clock. If he was still alive, I thought, Mom wouldn't have nightmares. The man who wrote those encouraging letters to Mom, at the same time he was writing in his journal how scared he was that he would never see us again, would know the right things to say to make her feel better.

I rubbed Mom's shoulders.

"I wish Rose was here," she said.

I wanted to say, "I wish Dad was here," but that would have just made things worse. Sometimes I wondered how I could miss Dad so much when I could hardly remember him.

"She'll be back tomorrow," I said. "Do you want to talk to Dr. Haas?" Aunt Rose had printed the doctor's number in big bold handwriting and pinned it to the lamp shade next to Mom's bed.

"No. I have an appointment tomorrow anyway." Mom rubbed her eyes. "I thought this job would help get rid of the nightmares."

"What were you dreaming about?" I asked.

"Shut up, Lisa," Jenny said from the doorway. I scowled at her. Aunt Rose and Dr. Haas had told me to encourage Mom to talk.

"It was just the thunder," Jenny said through gritted teeth. "It's that stupid Joe Hansen's fault."

She sat behind Mom on the bed and began massaging her neck. "If he hadn't caught that baseball with his face, Mom wouldn't have had a nightmare tonight."

"Don't be stupid, Jenny," I said. "Mom's seen worse things than Joe Hansen's eye."

"You know what I mean," Jenny said. Then she put her finger to her lips and glared at me. She was telling me to shut up again. Mom had her eyes closed and didn't even seem to hear us.

I did know what Jenny meant. Joe Hansen was in my seventh-grade homeroom at school. He was tall and looked more like an eighteen-year-old than the thirteen-year-old he was. My friend Heather and I both thought he was the best-looking guy in the school. He reminded me of the soldiers Mom had pictures of in the box—short hair, thin, tanned. Joe was a great athlete too, but while we were playing baseball during gym that afternoon, he stepped into a pitch. The ball hit him on the left side of his face and made a big gash under his eye. He was knocked out.

Someone ran to get Mom, who's the school nurse, and to call an ambulance. All the rest of us seventh graders stood and watched while Joe's eye puffed up and Mr. Hill, the gym teacher, tried to stop the bleeding. Everyone was too scared to move. We thought Joe might be dead the way he dropped like a rock when he got hit. Jenny's sixth-grade class came out while we were waiting for the ambulance. I told her what had happened.

Finally Mom came running across the grass playing field. Mom did all the right things. She checked his pulse. She looked at his eyes. She applied pressure to the cut. But she was white as a bedsheet, and her hands shook. The silly little cut that Joe had was nothing compared to what Mom must have seen in

Vietnam, or even what she'd seen in the emergency room where she used to work. So I figured the reason Mom looked like she was going to faint was that Joe reminded her of something or someone. I hoped Jenny and I were the only ones who noticed how bad she looked.

"Get the box out of the closet," Mom said suddenly, bringing me back to the present. Jenny sighed. I went and got the box.

Mom rummaged through the contents for a few minutes and then pulled out a picture that had one corner bent. She handed it to me. It was a picture of a young man sitting on top of a horse. I turned it over. "Me on Scarface. Summer 1966" it said in scraggly looking writing. Mom had written "Scott Boyd" at the bottom.

"He looks like Joe," I said.

Mom nodded. "I sat up with Scott one night in Vietnam. Writing letters for him to his mom and girlfriend. Keeping him company while he died."

I shivered. I didn't know what to say. But it didn't matter.

"I knew him pretty well by then," Mom went on. "He'd been wounded twice before. We always patched him up and sent him back out again. He gave me this picture that last night—so I wouldn't forget him." Mom took a deep breath and let it out. "As if I ever could."

She lay down on the bed. I put the picture in the box.

"At least Joe's okay," Jenny said, trying to sound cheerful.

"He didn't even have to spend the night in the hospital," I added.

Mom shuddered.

"Maybe I'll have to give up nursing altogether," she said.

She had left her job at the hospital emergency room when she first got depressed. This past fall she had decided to return to work and had taken a job at Whitney Avenue School. She'd been there almost nine months. Whitney Avenue School was private and expensive, but we didn't have to pay since Mom worked there. If Mom quit, Jenny and I would have to leave too.

I looked at Jenny and could see her lip start to tremble like she was going to cry. I didn't like the idea of leaving either. Still, I wasn't going to cry about something before it even happened. Jenny was always the dramatic one in the family.

"You aren't really going to give up nursing are you?" Jenny asked.

Mom shook her head. "No, I guess not. It's the only thing I know how to do," she said.

The hail outside had turned to rain again. I could barely hear it tapping on the window now. The thunder was a distant echo.

"You girls go back to bed. You've got school tomorrow," Mom said. "And I want to run before work." She pulled the covers up around her neck. We both kissed her good night. I turned out the light.

"Do you want the radio on?" I asked. Maybe it would keep her mind off things.

"Sure," she said. I pushed the sleep button and classical music filled the silence. I kissed her cheek again. She smiled without opening her eyes.

"Don't worry," she said. "I'm okay."

Back in my room, I lay holding Dad's dog tag tightly in my hand and prayed silently that Mom would sleep until morning.

But God wasn't listening. A while later Mom screamed. This time Jenny woke up right away too. We practically knocked each other over running down the hall.

"Robert! Robert!" Mom cried out.

I flipped on the light in her room and touched her arm. She was soaked with sweat.

Jenny's lip trembled again like she was going to cry. That was all I needed. "You're no help!" I shouted at her.

For a moment Mom looked wildly from me to Jenny.

"Mom," I said softly.

Her body sagged. She started breathing more easily.

"You were calling for Dad," I said.

"Shush, Lisa," Jenny hissed.

Mom stared at the ceiling.

"He was my patient and I let him die," Mom said.

"No, Mom. You were home taking care of us when Dad was killed in Vietnam," I said.

"I should have been there when he died. I should have been there."

I crawled into bed beside Mom then, and put my arm around her. After a while Jenny did too. It was what Aunt Rose would have done if she had been there. But that night it was only Jenny and me— spending the night with Mom in Vietnam.

# TWO

I always thought of that thunderstorm as the beginning. The beginning of Mom's depression.
Of course it wasn't. That had come the spring before when Mom was still working the ER.

One day a teenage boy was brought into the hospital DOA—dead on arrival. Mom started crying
when she saw him, and couldn't stop. Aunt Rose
had to bring her home. Mom stayed in bed for the
next two weeks—until Aunt Rose talked her into
seeing a psychiatrist. The following three months
Mom did little but eat and sleep. She never went
back to that job.

Even that day at the hospital probably wasn't the
start of Mom's problems. I wondered if it started
when Mom stayed up all night with Scott Boyd in

Vietnam—waiting for him to die. Or when Dad died. Aunt Rose said it was hard to tell.

Still, the thunderstorm was a kind of beginning for Jenny and me. It was the first time we had to comfort Mom on our own. And maybe the first time we understood how much pain she was going through.

From that night on, Mom treated us differently. It was as if all the walls she'd put up to keep us from her problems had suddenly fallen down. She told us over and over how sorry she was about being so messed up. We told her over and over that it was okay—but I know a part of me didn't mean it. I wanted to have a mom who took care of me and acted ordinary. I wanted to hang out with my friends and not feel like I had to see how she was doing all the time.

A month after that stormy night we finished out the year at Whitney Avenue School with a family picnic. Aunt Rose came with us and Mom seemed to have a good time. I spent most of the time playing softball with my friends Heather and Josh and a bunch of other seventh graders, but every once in a while I looked over and Mom was always talking to someone—a teacher or a parent.

Over the summer Mom and Aunt Rose drove Jenny and me to Orlando, Florida, for a couple of weeks. We all stayed with Aunt Rose and Mom's parents—my grandparents—who had a beautiful blue-tile swimming pool in their backyard. Mom said the Florida heat always reminded her of Vietnam. I thought everything reminded her of Vietnam, but I didn't say so.

Grandma and Grandpa didn't seem to know any-thing about Mom's depression. I think they knew that Mom still missed Dad—it would be hard not to notice that. It had been ten years since Dad died, and Mom had been out with maybe three men since, though never more than a few times with each of them. But I didn't think that Grandma and Grandpa understood that Mom missing Dad was only one part of the problem. She worked really hard to hide her emotions and act ordinary around them. If she was up in the middle of the night while we stayed with them, I never heard her.

We went to Disney World and Universal Studios and I sent postcards home to Heather and Josh and told them I was having a wonderful time—which I was. But to be truthful I was also waiting for some-thing to go wrong.

Those two weeks in Florida were the longest Mom had gone in over a year without having a session with Dr. Haas. By the time we left she was starting to do things that worried me, like pace the floor in the middle of the day and snap at us if we giggled too loudly in the car.

"Is your sister okay?" I overheard Grandma whisper to Aunt Rose one day.

"I think she's just anxious to get back to New Haven," Aunt Rose said.

Grandma nodded as if that was a good explanation.

"I know," Grandpa added. "That was home my whole life. I still miss it."

I wondered how they could believe homesickness was the only thing troubling Mom. Aunt Rose said maybe it was too hard for them to see the truth—which I didn't understand. When we left they smothered us with hugs and kisses and said they'd see us at Christmas.

We stopped in Chapel Hill, North Carolina, on the way back and stayed with Aunt Rose's old college professor Kathy Martin. Before Kathy was a professor she had been a reporter in Vietnam. Aunt Rose had wanted Mom to meet her.

Kathy and Mom had been in Vietnam at about

the same time. Kathy talked a lot about something called the Tet Offensive and about a city called
"Way." Mom didn't say much, but she seemed to
be listening.

"What was it like when you came home?" Kathy
asked.

"Ordinary," Mom said.

Kathy nodded.

"I know what you mean," Kathy said. "My sister
picked me up at the airport when I got back. She
was wearing an orange tank top and neon pink bell-
bottoms. We drove off in her little red MG, listening
to some bubble gum music on the radio." Kathy
leaned back on the couch and stared at the ceiling. "I
remember thinking—this is too ordinary—there's
no blood, no napalm, no rocket attacks, no gunfire,
no screaming children. And just a plane ride away, all
that was still going on. Men were still dying while I
was riding around in a convertible."

Mom took a sip of her Coke and stared at the
floor. "And I felt guilty that Robert—and everyone
else—was still over there and I was home," she added.

Kathy nodded.

"But Robert wanted to be there," Aunt Rose
said. I knew that was true. Dad had planned to make

the Army his career. He died on his fourth tour of duty in Vietnam.

"I know," Mom said. "But it didn't make me feel better."

"Did you ever join any veterans' groups?" Kathy asked.

Mom shook her head. "I tried to join in a Vietnam Veterans Against the War march once. But they wouldn't let me."

"Wouldn't let you?" Kathy asked.

"No," Mom said. "There were going to be a lot of TV cameras there and the organizers thought a woman marching wouldn't look real. The public wouldn't believe that a woman could be a Vietnam vet, they said."

I felt a rush of anger. "That stinks, Mom," I said. "I hope you yelled at somebody."

"I should have," Mom said. "But I was so shocked, I just walked away."

"That's one of the worst vet stories I've heard," Kathy said. "Those guys should have known better."

"What did Dad say?" I asked.

Mom laughed. "He was really steamed. Said he'd kick some butt when he came home next time on leave."

"Didn't he care that you were protesting the war?" I asked.

"No. By then he thought that the politicians in Washington were just sending boys over there to get killed. He wanted the war to end too, but he wasn't about to stay in the States and let those guys fight without him. Robert honestly felt he could keep some new grunt from getting killed if he was there to show him the ropes."

"He was probably right," Kathy said.

There was a long silence.

"I'm going to go back soon," Kathy finally said. "To Vietnam. Some other reporters—friends of mine—are getting together a tour group. You could come with us, Mary Ann."

An even longer silence followed. Jenny was asleep on the couch—or pretending to be. I lay in a huge, overstuffed chair. I closed my eyes while I waited to see what Mom would answer.

"I don't think I could . . ." Mom said. "Maybe . . ."

A look passed between Aunt Rose and Kathy. I wasn't sure what it meant, but Kathy changed the subject.

"Are you going to go to the dedication of the Wall?" Kathy asked.

For a change I actually knew what she was talking about. There was a monument being built in Washington, D.C., called the Vietnam Veterans Memorial. A student from Yale designed it, so it was pretty big news in New Haven, Connecticut. People had started calling it the Wall for short since that's what it was—a long black wall with the names of all the Americans who died or were missing in Vietnam carved into it. A wall with Dad's name on it somewhere.

I was surprised how loud and strong Mom's voice was when she replied.

"Of course I am," she said, and then looked from Jenny to me. "We all are."

I hadn't known until that moment that Mom was planning to take us to the dedication. I wondered how long Mom had been planning it, or if she'd made up her mind that very minute. It really didn't matter.

After we came home from our trip Aunt Rose got the idea to do a photo essay about the Wall and relate it to our family experience. So Vietnam started to be all she talked about too. She was always asking Mom questions. Sometimes Mom even seemed to like answering them.

The rest of the summer was pretty quiet and boring. Mom still paced around a lot at night. Aunt Rose didn't have to go away on any jobs all summer though, so I didn't have to think about Mom's problems much. But of course I did. It was hard not to worry.

Heather invited me to go swimming at the Lawn Club a couple of times and Josh invited me to a barbecue at his house. It would have been fun except that Joe Hansen was there with his family, and he made me so nervous, I couldn't eat.

When school finally started in the fall I was glad to have things to do that kept my mind off Mom, like homework, soccer games—and thinking about Joe Hansen. It was better than listening to Mom and Aunt Rose talk about Vietnam for the hundredth time. I once heard Mom tell Aunt Rose that she sometimes felt like she had never left Vietnam. That she was still there in her mind. Some days it felt like that to me too—as if both my parents had died.

I only had a couple of good friends and sometimes I had trouble talking even to them. Mom had been shy just like me when she was young, so she was the person I always talked to. I didn't stumble over my words with her, and even when I didn't say exactly what I meant, she understood. But when she got to thinking about Vietnam I couldn't talk to her. She didn't hear me. It made me lonely.

So when school started I was glad to escape the silence and the conversations about Vietnam. But then something happened to change everything.

 **Three**

"Hurry up, Jenny!" I called in a loud whisper. "We're late."

"I can't find my math homework," Jenny said from her room. I watched from the hall as a pillow flew out the door. Pieces of paper fluttered out, followed by a wad of dirty clothes and a couple of teddy bears. "Mrs. Donahue is going to kill me! I'm ruined! They'll probably kick me out of school!"

"Be quiet, Jenny. Mom's still trying to sleep," I said. Mom had had a sleepless night. I had heard her pacing upstairs on the third floor while she talked to Aunt Rose.

Jenny was frantically searching through the junk that surrounded her bed.

"Just explain that you lost your homework. You're

always exaggerating. They aren't going to kick you out," I said.

"That's easy for you to say," she said. "Miss Never-Lose-Your-Homework, Straight-A Student. They don't like me up there as much as they like you."

"Don't be stupid," I said. She wrinkled her nose at me. I followed her downstairs to the living room where she began looking under sofa cushions and newspapers.

"What's on the coffee table?" I asked.

"Aha," Jenny said. She pulled a wrinkled sheet of notebook paper out from under a *Newsweek.* "No wonder I couldn't find it. It was right where I left it."

I pushed her toward the front door. While she struggled to put her homework in her backpack, I heard someone come down the back stairs.

Aunt Rose waved from the kitchen doorway with one hand while she stifled a yawn with the other.

"Where's your mom?"

"Sleeping," I said. "I think she called in sick."

Aunt Rose frowned.

"I'll take her some coffee and see if I can get her to work. It will do her good."

"Maybe she should just sleep," I said.

"Yeah," Jenny added. "I think she's really tired."

"This coffee will get her going." Aunt Rose scooped spoonful after spoonful of ground coffee into the coffeemaker. I knew it was going to be way stronger than Mom made.

"Do you always make your coffee like that?" I asked.

"No. Only when I want to zap someone to life." Aunt Rose laughed. "This'll put hair on your chest."

Jenny giggled. "I don't think Mom would look too good with hair on her chest."

Aunt Rose laughed again. "You two better scoot to school or you're going to be late."

Jenny and I did as we were told.

"I wish Mom was more like Aunt Rose," Jenny said as we walked to school. I was startled to realize that I'd been thinking the same thing, and I felt instantly guilty and disloyal somehow.

"Jenny!" I said. "That's a terrible thing to say."

"Well, I don't care," she said. "At least Aunt Rose isn't having nightmares and . . . and other problems."

"Mom can't help having nightmares."

"She could if she wanted to!"

Right, I thought. Just like I could help being shy

if I wanted to. I didn't bother to say it out loud because Jenny would have said "exactly." She believed that a person could do whatever they put their mind to. They just had to want it bad enough. If I put my mind to it I could make ten friends in ten minutes, like Jenny, and get Joe Hansen to ask me to dance at the fall dance. Right.

Jenny kicked a Coke can that was in the middle of the sidewalk.

"It's not fair!" she said. "I don't want any more nights with Mom pacing around or screaming in her sleep."

Her eyes seemed about to flood over when she turned to look at me. It didn't make me mad like it sometimes did. For some reason she reminded me of the cute little kid that she used to be—all bubbly and happy, laughing all the time. She didn't laugh much lately. I put my arm around her skinny shoulders.

"I want what you want, Jenny," I said. "But Mom needs to work out the past so she can face the present. It happens to lots of people. Mom just happens to have Vietnam in her past. Some people have other things." Geez, I thought. I was beginning to sound just like Aunt Rose.

"It's been years since she was there. Years since Dad died—why is she still having trouble?"

"You've read Mom's journal—and Dad's. You know what they saw. Do you think *you* could ever forget that?"

Jenny shook her head.

"I guess not," she said. And then not wanting to give up so easily, added, "But I think you and Aunt Rose are just making everything worse by getting Mom to talk all the time."

"We are not making Mom worse."

How could I be making Mom worse? I always made sure we watched happy shows on TV. I only tuned the radio to the classical station so no sad songs would drift through the house. I helped with dinner every night so Mom could go on her second run of the day and maybe would be too tired to dream. I even closed my eyes when she looked at me sometimes so she wouldn't see Dad's blue eyes looking back at her.

"We're not making Mom worse," I repeated.

"Then why has she had so many more night-mares since she started seeing that stupid doctor?"

That was a hard question to answer. The same thing I wondered sometimes.

"Aunt Rose says she's always had nightmares—ever since she came back," I said. "She's just not afraid to let us know about them now."

"I wish I still didn't know about them," Jenny said. She gave the Coke can another good kick.

"Do you remember Dad?" she asked suddenly. Just like Mom, I thought. Talk about Vietnam, and sooner or later we get around to Dad.

I reached up and rubbed the chain around my neck that held Dad's dog tag. A couple of years ago Mom had told me I could have it and Jenny could have his medals. Jenny had put the medals away in her treasure drawer. I was never without Dad's dog tag, but did I remember him?

When I thought of Dad I pictured a big tanned man and cigarettes that made me sneeze and the way he laughed when I tried to tickle him. His face smiled with deep dimples just like Jenny's. I didn't know if I really remembered all that or had just made up memories from the photos I'd seen and the stories Mom had told me.

"Maybe," I finally answered.

"At least Dad touched you," she said. "All he ever knew about me were some dumb photos. I look like I have a pointed head in those pictures."

"You do have a pointed head," I teased.

Jenny pushed me into the bushes we were walking beside.

"I hate it when you tease me when I'm trying to be serious," she said. Then she strode on ahead of me.

"Sorry," I called. But Jenny wasn't in the mood to listen to anything else I said.

When I got to school I felt better. I always did. I loved school. It was the place where I could go and count on the same things happening every day no matter what. We might go on field trips or have special programs, but the teachers told you about them ahead of time. At school I knew what to expect. There were no surprises. And no one ever talked about Vietnam.

I loved the first step into the hallway. Words filled the air. Ordinary, everyday talk.

"Hey, Cindy, did you do your algebra?"

"What did you get on problem number three?"

"Did you see what Wilson is wearing today?"

"Hey, we have a sub."

"Not again!"

I loved every word. Some days I wrote down everything I heard in my notebook just so I could read it over again at night. So I could feel ordinary again when I needed to.

At my locker Josh Steinberg came up and stood beside me, waiting. Josh had been my friend since the first day of seventh grade. Actually, even before, since we'd been friends in first and second grade at my old school. He was the kind of kid that always had the answers to the teachers' questions, even when it seemed like he hadn't studied. It didn't make him very popular. He got called "nerd" a lot, but I liked him.

He had dark curly hair that went in all directions, and gold wire-rimmed glasses. I thought he was cute and I probably would have been in love with him if it hadn't been for Joe Hansen.

After I got my books Josh and I headed down the hall together toward homeroom.

"Hey, Lisa," Heather called. "Wait up."

Heather was my other good friend at school. I'm slow to make friends, but Heather's not. She'd been my friend almost as long as Josh. Now that we were in eighth grade I felt like I'd known them both my whole life. I hadn't told either of them about Mom, but I almost had a few times. Especially when I was feeling lonely.

"Did you get your English done?" Josh asked.

"Yeah," I said. "I don't think it's right, though."

"I'm sure mine isn't," Heather said.

In homeroom Heather and I sat down at a table next to one another and waited for roll call. Josh sat across from me. Joe Hansen was there, looking gorgeous as usual.

Heather sighed. "My parents are such jerks."

"What did they do this time?" I asked. Heather was always complaining about them. Josh grinned at me.

"Last night Dad was stuck at the lab running an experiment and Mom was working on a story for the *Register*," Heather said. "They each thought the other one was home with me. They were still fighting when I left this morning." She smirked. "I hope they keep it up all morning. It will make up for last night. I was so mad at them. But I'm over it."

"You don't sound over it," Josh said.

Heather ignored him.

"If it happens again call me," I finally said. I wanted to add "you can come over," but I didn't think that would be a good idea. I didn't want my friends to start thinking Mom was crazy.

"If it happens again," Heather said, "I'll ask your mom to adopt me." All families had problems, I guessed.

Mom came to work later that day. She smiled and waved to me when I passed her office on the way to history class.

I loved history and Mr. Cooke was my favorite teacher. He made history exciting by letting us hear about different times in the words of the people who lived through them.

We were going to begin studying the founding of New Haven soon. Mr. Cooke was going to take us to the Historical Society to read letters and journals written by the colonists hundreds of years ago. I couldn't wait.

Next term we were going to study twentieth-century America and Heather said we would get to see all kinds of documentary films. Her cousin had been in Mr. Cooke's class two years before and she told Heather it was great.

"Class," Mr. Cooke began, "today we are going to begin a month-long study of the war in Vietnam."

I felt as though someone had kicked me in the stomach. For a minute I couldn't breathe. Then I took a deep breath and let it out. I pulled Dad's dog tag out and held it pressed between my hands. This couldn't be happening.

"I usually wait until the end of the year to start

on this topic. But the Vietnam Veterans Memorial will be dedicated in two months. As you probably know, Maya Lin designed it when she was a student at Yale right here in New Haven. It will be a wall with the names of over 58,000 Americans killed or missing in Vietnam."

Of course I knew all of this already. You couldn't very well live at my house and not know about the Wall.

"My dad said this woman designed it for a class and only got a B on it," Joe said. A couple of boys next to him snickered.

"That's right," Mr. Cooke said. "She only made a B with this design. But I hope you won't take that to mean that your papers will someday win the Pulitzer, Mr. Hansen." Joe's cheeks got red and everyone laughed. Except me.

"Mrs. Smyth will be asking you to design your own memorial in art class," Mr. Cooke went on. "Ms. Levine will have you read and discuss a book by a marine who was there."

I didn't hear much after that. They were still just ordinary, everyday words. Something about speakers coming to our class to talk—a soldier, a war protester—and papers due on some aspect of the war, and on and on. I found no comfort in their sound anymore. I wanted to have a tantrum right there in the middle of history class just like Jenny might. I remembered Jenny's words that morning.

"It's not fair!" I yelled.

Everyone turned to stare at me.

# Four

"Excuse me, Lisa?" Mr. Cooke looked straight at me.

I felt my face get hot all the way up through my hair. Joe Hansen was staring right at me, grinning. Several kids giggled in the back. I had never said anything in class before except to answer questions.

Heather put her hand on my shoulder. Josh looked at me too and frowned like he was trying to figure out what had gotten into me.

"What's wrong?" Heather whispered.

I didn't answer.

"Lisa?" Mr. Cooke asked again.

"I . . . I need to talk to you," I said.

"Can it wait till after class?"

I nodded. I bent my head over my notebook

and began to doodle with my right hand. My left hand still held tightly to Dad's dog tag. Mr. Cooke continued with his talk on Vietnam. I didn't listen.

Surely Mr. Cooke would understand about this, I thought. I would tell him Dad was killed in the war. I'd tell him that Aunt Rose was doing a photo piece about the Wall and that I listened to Vietnam talk continuously at my house. I wouldn't tell him about Mom. Since she hadn't told anyone at the hospital, I didn't think she'd want the people at school to know either.

I was sure if I explained that I already knew all about Vietnam, Mr. Cooke would understand. I just knew he would let me go to the library every day for the next month instead of going to his class. I would volunteer to do a research project about ancient Greece or Rome. That's what I'd do. This would be the perfect solution. Mr. Cooke would agree. He had to.

"I'll save you a seat in French class, Lisa," Heather said, standing beside me. I looked up, startled, from my notebook.

"Thanks," I said. Then she smiled and hurried off. I slipped Dad's dog tag back inside my shirt.

Class was over. I was sitting alone in the room with Mr. Cooke.

"Yes, Lisa?" Mr. Cooke asked.

I looked down at my desk.

"I'd like to be excused from class for the next month," I said. "While you study Vietnam."

"Why is that?" Mr. Cooke asked. At least he hadn't said no right off. I supposed that was something.

"My father was killed in Vietnam," I said. "I already know as much as I need to know about the war. My aunt Rose—my mom's sister—is doing a photo essay about the Wall too. She's always talking about Vietnam. And my aunt's friend . . . a college professor . . . she told me all about the war. She was a reporter there. In Vietnam, I mean. I really don't want to hear about Vietnam anymore."

"I can understand that, Lisa," Mr. Cooke said. "I didn't realize your father was killed there. When did he die?"

"September tenth, 1971," I said.

"You were very young. Do you remember him?"

I shook my head.

"His name will be on the memorial."

I nodded.

Mr. Cooke cleared his throat. "Lisa, the Vietnam

War is a very complicated subject. I'm sure you will find out things you never knew from my class."

"I doubt it," I answered. I couldn't believe I'd actually said that to a teacher. I didn't look at him, but I heard him sigh.

"Okay, Lisa. I'll give you a pop quiz," he said. "Tell me what president took most of the heat for our involvement in Vietnam."

"Lyndon Johnson," I answered. "People were so mad at him that he didn't run for a second term."

Mr. Cooke nodded.

"Good. And what about the draft? How did men avoid being drafted?"

"Well," I started. "Some men got married and had kids, some went to college, and when all else failed, some men ran away to Canada." I thought Aunt Rose and her professor would have been glad to know I was paying such close attention.

"What was the Hanoi Hilton?" he asked quickly.

"A prison in Hanoi, North Vietnam, where the North Vietnamese held prisoners of war."

"Tell me about 'Way,' " he said next. Then he wrote it on the blackboard—Hue. I hadn't known it was spelled like that, but I did know it was a town in Vietnam. So that's what I said.

"But what happened there?" he asked.

I didn't know the answer.

"What about My Lai? Have you learned about that?"

I shook my head. I guessed that I wouldn't be getting out of his class.

"You do know a lot, Lisa," Mr. Cooke said. "But there is still a lot left for you to learn. I feel like our class has been given a gift—you. You are going to be able to add so much!"

I knew he was trying to be nice and get me interested, but he was just making me mad. I didn't want to give his class anything.

"You don't really want to sit out a whole month of school, do you? We'd miss you."

I opened my mouth to speak, but no words came out. I had no idea what to say. Mr. Cooke looked at his watch.

"I have to run to a meeting," he said. "I'll walk with you to your next class."

We stepped into the hall. Under normal circumstances I would have been happy that Mr. Cooke wanted to walk with me, but I wasn't. I wondered if after that day I would ever like him again.

"My friend Matt was in Vietnam. He's going to

come and talk to the class in a couple of weeks. Do you think your aunt and her friend could come and talk to the class?" he asked.

"My aunt probably could," I said. "But her friend lives in North Carolina and I don't know if she'd want to drive all that way."

"She was a reporter there?"

I nodded.

"Maybe we could send her some questions and she could write us a letter, or better yet, get someone to tape her answers."

"Maybe . . ."

"Do you know when she was there?"

"I think about 1968," I said. "The same time as Mom."

I put my hand over my mouth. I couldn't believe how easily those words had come out. Somehow with me words either slipped out when I didn't want them to, or came out all jumbled and confused.

"Your mom was there?" he asked.

"Well—um—yes," I said. "But she . . ." I started to say she didn't like to talk about it all that much, but that wasn't really true and I didn't know how to explain it all in the two minutes I had before French class.

"Was she a nurse there?" he asked and then

without waiting for an answer he rushed on. "She must have been. This could be great. She could give the class her ideas about the war."

"I don't think Mom would want to do that," I finally managed to say.

"Oh?" Mr. Cooke's eyebrows went up.

Again I didn't know what to say. It would be hard for her, but she was supposed to talk about it, that's what Dr. Haas and Aunt Rose said anyway. But I couldn't explain all that to Mr. Cooke.

We passed by Mom's office then. It turned out that Mr. Cooke wasn't in as much of a hurry as he'd said. He stopped at Mom's open door and knocked on the door frame. Mom looked up from her desk and smiled.

"Maybe I should just ask her," he whispered. He didn't wait for me to say anything.

"Mary Ann," he said, "my eighth-grade class is beginning a study of the war in Vietnam. Lisa tells me you were there. I was wondering if you and your sister—" he turned to look at me, "who is planning a photo essay about the Wall, right?" I nodded. He turned back to Mom. "I wondered if the two of you could come and talk to my class. I'd particularly like your view. You know the perspective of someone who was in Vietnam during the war but who wasn't part of the warfare. Give the kids the other side of war."

Mom stared at him. She didn't answer. Mr. Cooke shifted his weight to his right foot and jingled the keys in his pocket.

"If you'd rather not . . ." he said.

Mom looked into her desk drawer for a moment then closed it.

"I'll have to think about it," she said.

"Sure," Mr. Cooke said. "Let me know."

Mr. Cooke turned, bumped into me, and then walked hurriedly down the hall. Mom stood up from her desk and looked out the window. I came in and closed the door behind me.

"Not 'part of the warfare' . . ." Mom repeated Mr. Cooke's words.

"Are you mad at me, Mom?" I asked. "I didn't mean to tell him. It just sort of slipped out when he started talking about Vietnam."

"I'm not mad at you, Lisa," she said. "I'm mad at myself."

"Why?"

She turned around and smiled at me for a minute. Then she sat back down at her desk.

"I wish I hadn't been quiet all these years." She gestured toward the door with her thumb. "He certainly has no idea what it was like for women in Vietnam."

"Maybe you should tell him," I said.

She looked up and stared out the window.

"Should I tell him?" she said. "Should I tell him about the men with no arms and legs, or the men with holes in their stomachs who came to us conscious and so sure that we could make them okay again? Should I tell him how the first time I saw a room full of casualties I thought I would never make it through the day without passing out or throwing up? Should I talk about the buckets of body parts we buried every day?"

Mom looked at me then. I shivered.

"Not part of the warfare? He's an idiot," she said.

"I know," I said. "But it's not his fault he doesn't know what it was like. Talk to him and see what he says."

"I used to want to talk about what it was like," she said. "When I first came back. But when I brought it up people would look at me like they just wanted me to go away. So I stopped."

"Couldn't you talk to Aunt Rose or Grandma and Grandpa?"

"Your aunt Rose was too young to talk to then. Your grandmother said my stories were too horrible to listen to, but your grandfather seemed to want to hear all about people I'd been close to who had died. I never really understood why. They both just made me want to scream. I was glad when they finally moved to Florida.

"Some of my friends would ask polite questions, but they would change the subject if I told them too much. So I finally decided not to talk about it to anyone. Ever. I decided to forget."

"How did you ever think you could forget?" I asked.

"I don't know. I only know that I couldn't forget. And now I realize that I don't want to forget." She tapped her forehead. "I have too many souls in here." She put her hand over her heart. "And in here. They deserve remembering. I'm not going to shut them out anymore."

"What about Mr. Cooke?" I asked.

"I'll talk to him today or call him tonight," she said. "I'll see what he says. Maybe he'll decide he'd rather not have me talk to your class. That would make it easy."

"Right," I said. She looked at me, then came over and gave me a hug. That's what I liked about Mom. She knew exactly what I meant without me explaining it—that nothing about Vietnam was ever easy.

Five

"Pizza, pizza! Get it while it's hot!" Aunt Rose came through the swinging door to our kitchen where I was doing my homework. She was carrying two pizza boxes in her arms. She dropped them right onto my math book.

"You're back!" I said. I jumped up to hug Aunt Rose. She had been gone for five days in Washington, D.C., to do some research on the Wall.

"I missed you guys," she said as she hugged me back. "Where is everyone?"

"Mom's gone for a run and Jenny is sulking in her room—boy problems, I think," I said. "How did you know we hadn't eaten supper already?"

"I know this family," she said, smiling. "You're lucky to get fed by eight o'clock. Besides, I've been craving Modern's pizza while I was away, and if you had all been too full to eat, I would've eaten it by myself." Modern was the name of our favorite pizza place.

"*Mmmmm,*" Aunt Rose said. She took a slice of pizza, tipped her head back, and bit into it. She leaned against the countertop and closed her eyes while she chewed. I laughed.

She opened her eyes and frowned at me. "Someday you'll be without Modern's pizza for a whole week and we'll see how you hold up," she said, and then laughed too. "So, what happened while I was gone?"

"Not much," I said. "Mom hasn't called Mr. Cooke yet."

"You think I should suggest we do our presentations together?"

"Maybe," I said. I didn't really know if anything would get Mom to talk to my class. Besides, I had problems of my own. There was the upcoming fall dance and also a little problem of designing a Vietnam veterans memorial for art class. I had no idea what to do about either.

"Hello? Hello?" Aunt Rose waved a slice of pizza on a plate in front of my face. "Earth to Lisa. Do you want some pizza?"

"Sorry," I said, taking the plate from her. "I was thinking."

"That's a novel idea." She grinned and handed me a can of Coke. "What about?"

I sighed and took a bite of pizza.

"Too private to talk about?" Aunt Rose asked.

"Not really," I answered. "I have a couple of problems. The first one is that I promised Heather I'd go to the fall dance and I don't know how to dance."

"Of course you know how," Aunt Rose said. "You just haven't tried."

Boy, did that sound like Jenny. "Anything is possible—you just have to try." Right. All of a sudden I wished I hadn't said anything.

"Come on," Aunt Rose said, grabbing my hand. "Let's go practice."

"Aw, Aunt Rose," I grumbled. "It's hopeless." To tell the truth, I was embarrassed to try dancing even in front of Aunt Rose. I looked like an idiot whenever I tried.

"Nothing is hopeless," Aunt Rose said.

She shuffled through Mom's old record collection and came out with a Crosby, Stills, Nash and Young album. She put it on the turntable and cranked the volume way up.

Jenny came downstairs just as Aunt Rose started dancing—hopping around and swinging her arms.

"See, anyone can dance," she shouted above the music.

I looked at Jenny and we both burst out laughing. Aunt Rose smiled and kept dancing.

"Get moving, you guys," she said.

I started trying to copy my aunt's moves. Jenny did too. We all looked ridiculous. Jenny had already been to some dances the year before. I'd always found an excuse not to go. The truth was I couldn't decide which would be worse, being asked to dance or not being asked.

Aunt Rose grabbed Jenny by the hand and they did some twists and turns together. While they were dancing Mom came back from her run and stood watching us in the doorway. Pretty soon she took my hand and we were dancing like Jenny and Aunt Rose.

"Get down, big sister," Aunt Rose said. Mom let go of my hand and started dancing by herself. She was way better than Aunt Rose.

"Hey," I said. "I thought you said you were too shy to go to dances when you were young."

"I was. But that didn't stop me from watching

*American Bandstand* and dancing in front of the mirror."

We danced through two more songs before Aunt Rose stopped us.

"Pizza break!" she said. We all sat down on the floor right where we were and Aunt Rose brought us plates of pizza.

But of course nothing ever stayed calm in our house for long. While I was eating I remembered about my art project.

"Mom, can I look through the Vietnam box?" I started. "I need to—"

"Of course," Mom said, cutting me off. "You don't need to ask permission. Look at those things anytime you want."

"Can't we ever go ten minutes around here without somebody bringing up Vietnam?" Jenny asked. She got up and stomped into the kitchen. I heard her plate clunk on the counter. Then I heard her angry footsteps on the back staircase, followed by the slam of her bedroom door.

Mom and Aunt Rose exchanged a glance that I was surprised to see looked amused. Was that a good sign?

In Mom's room I went to the closet, pulling

Mom's desk chair with me. I climbed up on the chair and lifted the big box down from the top of the closet. My hand brushed against the smooth fabric of the folded flag sitting next to it on the shelf. Dad's flag—the one they covered his coffin with. The one the two soldiers folded into a triangle and gave to Mom on the day of his funeral. I didn't remember it, but I knew that's what happened at a soldier's funeral.

Mom came in to take a shower. Out in the hall I heard Aunt Rose knock softly on Jenny's door. I started going through the box. I hadn't really looked through it in a long time.

I wondered if I could get an idea from this heap of memories. There were two journals, two stacks of letters, a faded green army cap, and lots of photographs. Some of the pictures were in color. Others were in black and white. Some had names and dates written on the back. Most had nothing written on them at all. None of them seemed to be in any kind of order.

I could hear Aunt Rose's voice getting louder, saying things like "Quit being so selfish" and "Give your mom your support even if it means talking about Vietnam all the time."

"I don't want to talk about it anymore!" Jenny finally screamed. And then her door slammed again.

I lifted a stack of pictures from the box and started going through them. Most of the people and places were unfamiliar. There were several of Mom with other women. It looked like they were nurses too. I wondered where those women were. Did they have children that would listen when they talked about Vietnam?

The pictures I was holding were in color, but they might as well have been in black and white. Everything was green and brown—the uniforms of the soldiers and nurses, the trees and buildings.

I picked up another stack. In one picture a little girl hugging a teddy bear was being held by a big nurse wearing a green cap and a wide grin. The girl's arms were bandaged. Another picture was of five little boys holding up toy cars and smiling as if they were all trying to say "cheese" for the camera.

The last picture in the stack was of Mom and Dad before they were married standing with two Vietnamese girls in the middle of a muddy road. The older girl stood straight in front of Dad. He had his hand on her shoulder and she hugged a book to her chest. The younger girl was turned sideways, leaning into Mom. She also had a book. They were all smiling. On the back was written Christmas 1968—right after my parents met.

I stared at that picture for a long time. Mom looked so young and happy. Dad looked young too. So much younger than he looked in the pictures taken during his fourth year—the tour of duty in which he was killed.

I was about to put the picture back in the box. Then I looked at it again. It made me mad. Here was a picture of two girls who were about the same age as Jenny and me. They were smiling for the camera on a Christmas long ago with my parents. Jenny and I should have had the chance to stand like that with our parents on Christmas Day. We never had. We never would.

I kept staring at the picture and suddenly I had an idea for my art project.

I was so excited about my idea that I wanted to tell Jenny. I ran to her room. She was lying on her bed looking at the ceiling.

"Look, Jenny!" I said. "Look at this great picture I found. . . ."

Jenny stared at the picture and before I could even start telling her about my idea, she jumped up and grabbed it from me.

"No one ever listens to me!" she shouted.

"Jenny, stop!" I yelled. But it was too late. She had torn the picture in two. When I picked up the pieces I found that the faces weren't damaged. But my parents were now alone in one half of the picture and the two girls were alone in the other.

## Six

I didn't speak to Jenny for three days—that is, after I'd called her every bad name I could think of and asked Mom to ground her for the rest of her life. Mom gave her a week, but for Jenny a week was forever.

I waited in suspense during those three days while Aunt Rose tried to repair the damage. Finally one day after school she handed me two photographs. The original was on top—repaired so well that the rip was almost invisible. The other picture was a copy of the repaired photo and the rip *was* invisible on that one.

"Wow, thanks," I said. "How did you do it?"

"I am pretty talented, aren't I?" Aunt Rose said with a grin. "First I repaired the original that Miss

Hothead tried to ruin." She looked over at Jenny reading a book on the couch. Jenny ignored her.

"After that," Aunt Rose went on, "it was a matter of shooting a couple of pictures and making a new print for you."

"Thanks," I said. "Now we can get started on my project."

"I've been thinking about that," Aunt Rose said, sitting down beside me on the love seat. "I think the less of my help you use, the better."

"But . . ." I started to protest. I was really counting on her to help me do this right.

"Just listen a minute. If I do it, it will look professional."

"I want it to look good," I insisted.

"It will," Aunt Rose replied. "Trust me."

"Will you at least make copies for me when I'm done?"

"Of course," she said.

"I think *you* owe me a thank you too," Aunt Rose said, poking a finger in Jenny's side. Jenny tried not to smile. She put a pillow over her face. It was strange, but tearing the picture had let out a lot of Jenny's anger. She didn't get so mad when we talked about Vietnam anymore.

"Thank you." Jenny's voice came out muffled from behind the pillow.

"That's not much of a thank you for someone who saved your life," I said.

Jenny moved the pillow and looked right at Aunt Rose.

"Okay, okay," Jenny said. "Thank you from the bottom of my heart, Aunt Rose. Now will one of you ask Mom if I can get out early for good behavior?"

"Sorry," Aunt Rose and I said together. We both laughed. Jenny laughed too, but threw a sofa pillow at us anyway.

Even with the Jenny incident, I was starting to feel better about my problems. I had an art project to work on and I thought I might even make it through my first dance.

Mom finally called Mr. Cooke too. They agreed she would come and talk to my class in a couple of weeks. Aunt Rose would come too, another day, and show pictures of the Wall being built.

Mr. Cooke made the announcement about it in class, so thanks to him every kid in eighth-grade history now knew that my father had died and my mom had been a nurse in Vietnam.

"How come you never told me?" Heather whispered during class.

Josh looked over at us and I knew he was wondering the same thing. I didn't know what to say, so I just shrugged. How could I explain that Mom and I were just beginning to talk about it? How could I explain that it was the war that put our family together *and* tore it apart?

"Your art project is going to be great, I bet," Josh said later in the hall.

"I don't know," I replied. "I'm not a very good artist."

"Do you know what you're going to do?" Heather asked.

I nodded.

"Well?" Josh persisted.

"I'll show you when I'm done," I said. "Promise."

Heather leaned over and talked to Josh like I wasn't there.

"She is starting to get on my nerves," she said.

Josh grinned.

I knew she was teasing. But I also knew that it was partly true.

A few days before we started to work on our art projects at school, Mrs. Smyth showed us slides of war memorials around the world and told us what the artists had been trying to accomplish.

While a drawing of the Vietnam Veterans Memorial was projected, Mrs. Smyth said, "Maya Lin wanted to cut open the ground like a wound to express the sadness of losing a loved one. She also wanted to symbolize the wall between the living and the dead." Mrs. Smyth said that the Wall would be polished granite so that the living would be reflected in it.

Later we went on a walk to Woolsey Hall at Yale to look at the war memorial there. When we arrived we could hear someone playing the giant pipe organ inside the concert hall. The music sounded like something from a horror movie.

We walked through the circular main lobby and into a smaller lobby just outside the concert hall. The music was even louder there. The walls were lined with the names of Yale graduates who had died in war. Mrs. Smyth pointed out the list of those who had died in Vietnam. It was a short list and ran down the inside of a thick marble door frame.

I stood reading the names long after everyone else had wandered off.

Marlin, McClelland Miller 1968, I read. 1968—the

year he graduated from Yale, I figured. 1st Lieutenant Infantry, USA, June 20, 1971, Vietnam. I was pretty sure what all that meant. Rank, United States Army, date killed, somewhere in Vietnam. Some of the lines after other men's names were more specific about where the man was killed—near Hung Nhon, one said. Still, it wasn't much to know about someone.

I wondered if these men looked like the ones Mom had pictures of in the box. I hoped that wherever their families were, they had big boxes of memories in the tops of their closets just like we did.

# Seven

A few days later Mr. Cooke's friend Matt Parker came to talk to our class. I watched him as he walked down the hall with Mr. Cooke. He was tall and used a cane to balance himself with one hand. Mr. Cooke wheeled a cart with a slide projector on it. I wondered if Matt Parker's experiences would be anything like Dad's.

Mr. Parker stood in front of the class and introduced himself.

"My name is Matt Parker," he said. "I'm an assistant history professor at Yale. I've known your teacher since we were about two years old. We grew up together right here in New Haven.

"I was a marine from 1968 until 1971," Mr. Parker continued. "Most of that time was spent in

Vietnam at a place called An Hoa, which is near Da Nang." He held up a map and showed us the places near the top of a long, skinny country. Then he held up the brown wooden cane in his hand.

"I use this cane because a land mine exploded under me during my last month in Vietnam." Then he lifted the legs of his pants to show us two plastic limbs starting just below the knees. "The same mine killed three of my friends. I promised to buy those guys an ice-cold beer when we returned home. A few minutes after I made that promise we tripped a mine." He stopped and cleared his throat. "I guess that was about the last thing I ever said to them. Vietnam wasn't the kind of place where you got to have long good-byes."

The room was as silent as I'd ever heard it. I looked at Matt Parker's legs and couldn't believe he was able to walk around at all. I felt queasy imagining how he must have looked when he first got to a hospital. A hospital like the one Mom worked in.

"I can answer any questions you have about my injuries later," he said. "But first I'll show some slides and tell you more about what the war was like."

Mr. Parker's slides were of a better quality than

Mom's pictures. He had shots of his first day in Vietnam, some enemy traps that he found on patrol, his vacation to Australia, and finally two pictures of dead Vietnamese people. Mom didn't have any like that.

One slide showed a village with a lone chicken perched on a fence post, its wings spread as though it were about to flap away from the photographer. Beyond that were bodies lining the dirt lane leading through the village of thatched huts. I didn't look at it long enough to count the bodies, but there were many. Some of them were children. Who could do such a terrible thing?

"Vietcong did this," Mr. Parker said.

"I read that Americans killed innocent people too," Josh spoke up.

I sat up straighter in my chair. I was sure that Mr. Parker would be angry at the question. But he seemed ready for it.

"You're right," Mr. Parker said. "It did happen. Lots of horrifying things happen in war. Anytime you get soldiers that are exhausted and scared to death, some innocent people are going to get killed. But sometimes too those people aren't as innocent as they seem."

"What do you mean?" Josh asked.

Mr. Parker went on talking about how the Vietcong, the enemy, recruited old women, and children younger than us to throw grenades at soldiers, or worse. I quit listening after a while. I just wanted him to hurry and get to the next slide. I didn't want to look anymore.

While I tried not to listen to Mr. Parker, I thought about Dad. I wondered if the person who shot him saw his face. I wondered if that person imagined, even for an instant, that Robert Grey might have a wife and children waiting for him at home.

Then I started wondering who Dad had shot—not just who, but how many. And how many lonely widows and children were his fault? I didn't like thinking about that and I wished Mr. Parker would quit talking and leave so I could shut it all out.

Finally Mr. Cooke pushed the button in his hand and another slide dropped into the projector.

"This was my last stop in Vietnam—the evac hospital at Pleiku," Mr. Parker said.

It showed a room full of bandaged soldiers lying on beds set against the wall. Some were looking at the camera smiling, others couldn't. There was a nurse standing at the back of the room waving.

"I didn't take this picture," he added. "A friend of mine did since I was in no condition to care about picture taking. I was only there long enough to catch a helicopter out."

"Hey, Lisa," Joe joked, "is that your mom back there?"

"Shut up," Josh said.

I felt Mr. Parker looking straight at me.

"Your mom was in Vietnam?" he asked.

Mr. Cooke interrupted before I could say anything.

"This is Lisa Grey, the girl I was telling you about, Matt. Her father was killed in Vietnam and her mother was a nurse there."

"I'm sorry about your father," he said. "We lost a lot of good people over there."

"I know," I whispered.

Mr. Parker kept staring at me and no one else said anything either. I wished he'd get on with his talk. Finally he asked, "Where was your mom stationed?"

"Chu Lai," I said.

"I'd like to meet her."

"Lisa can show you where her office is when class is over," Mr. Cooke volunteered cheerfully.

Oh, thanks a lot, Mr. Cooke, I thought. What would coming face-to-face with a disabled vet do to Mom?

Mr. Parker spent the next fifteen minutes answering questions about the war. I sat and worried.

When he was done the whole class clapped. He smiled, and bowed stiffly.

"I'll take the slides out to your car if you want to go meet Mary Ann," Mr. Cooke said.

Mr. Parker nodded, then turned to me.

"Lead the way," he said.

We walked without talking down the hall. The hallways were filled with laughing, shouting kids going from one class to another. I wished that I was one of them. We finally arrived at Mom's open office door.

"Mom," I said. "This is Mr. Parker. He was in Vietnam. You know—he talked to our class today." I stumbled over what I was trying to say. "He wanted to meet you."

Mom got up from her desk and came over to Mr. Parker with her hand stretched out. He took her hand and shook it for a long time.

"I'm happy to meet you," she said. I could tell she really meant it.

"I'm glad to meet you too," he said. "I haven't had the chance to meet many nurses since I've been home. Here, watch this."

He walked to the door and then back to Mom.

Mom leaned her head to one side and frowned—looking at Mr. Parker's legs. She looked up at his face.

"You're an amputee!" Mom said with much more enthusiasm than I would have thought was right.

Mr. Parker lifted both legs of his pants to show her what he'd already shown our class.

"Oh!" Mom exclaimed. She put her hands up to her face and tears welled up in her eyes, but somehow she still looked happy.

"If it hadn't been for nurses like you, I'd be dead," he said. He smiled a big grin at Mom. "And look at me. I'm doing all right, aren't I? I just wanted to say thanks."

Then Mom hugged Mr. Parker, practically a stranger, right there in the middle of her office.

# Eight

Mr. Parker came over for supper that night. I'd never seen Mom so happy. As soon as school was out she made Jenny and me go with her to Prime Market to shop for London broil, potatoes, salad, and rolls. For a change she was going to do the cooking. While we were standing at the meat counter waiting for the butcher to wrap up a large package of beef, Mom asked, "What do you think about vanilla ice cream with homemade hot fudge sauce?"

"Yum!" Jenny said.

"I think Mr. Parker should come to dinner every night," I said.

Mom laughed.

When we got home I set the table and washed

the lettuce for the salad while Mom took a shower. Jenny did her homework in the living room.

"Hey, why don't you come and help me?" I yelled to Jenny.

"I don't know how to cook," she griped.

"You don't have to know how to cook," I countered. "I'll tell you what to do."

Jenny didn't answer me. I knew she hated doing things in the kitchen. Even when Mom and I made chocolate chip cookies, Jenny's favorite, the only thing Jenny ever wanted to do was pour in the chocolate chips.

I stood in the kitchen doorway and looked at my sister.

"At least come and chop up some onions for me," I said.

"Okay, okay," Jenny said.

While Jenny chopped I turned on the oven and started putting rolls out on a cookie sheet. Mom came downstairs with a towel wrapped around her head.

"How's it going?" she asked.

"Great," Jenny said. She sniffled. "Lisa is torturing me."

"Complain, complain, complain," I murmured.

Jenny stuck her tongue out at me. Her eyes were red and watery.

"I see that everything is business as usual," Mom teased. "I'll dry my hair and be right back to fix the rest of the dinner."

After Mom was gone the front door slammed and Aunt Rose called out, "Hello!"

"In the kitchen," I yelled.

Aunt Rose came in with a big potted plant in one arm and a bunch of purple and white flowers in the other.

"Flowers for the table," she said. "And an impulse purchase." It looked like Mom had called Aunt Rose about Matt Parker coming for dinner.

Jenny dumped the onions into the salad bowl as Mom came back into the kitchen.

"I've done my duty," Jenny said. She sprinted back into the living room.

"You have too, Lisa," Mom said. "Thanks for getting things started. I can do the rest."

I poured myself a Coke, then started putting the flowers into a vase.

"Those are really nice, Rose," Mom said. "Thanks."

Aunt Rose smiled.

"Now, I want you to be on your best behavior

tonight," Mom said. I thought she meant me and Jenny, but when I turned around I saw that she was looking at Aunt Rose.

"What?" Aunt Rose asked innocently.

"You know what I mean," Mom warned. "I don't want you to start snapping pictures of Matt just because he's a vet. At least let him get in the door first."

"I always let the guests in the door. Don't I, Lisa?" Aunt Rose asked.

"Don't give me any trouble," Mom said. She laughed and shook her finger at her sister.

Aunt Rose laughed too. "Boy, your mom is bossy," she said to me.

While Aunt Rose went up to the third floor to change clothes, Mom popped a tape into the cassette player on the kitchen counter. Soon I could hear Credence Clearwater Revival wailing about "Proud Mary." They were a group that Mom listened to a lot while she was in Vietnam.

I did my homework next to Jenny in the living room. When I was finished I got up to see if Mom wanted any more help. The smell of warm chocolate made my mouth water and I stopped at the kitchen doorway. Mom had her back to me. She was standing next to the stove and dancing as she stirred the fudge sauce.

I got a lump in my throat that I tried to swallow away. Seeing her dance like that made me picture the shy girl she said she was when she was my age, dancing alone in front of the mirror. I knew that she went dancing with Dad a couple of times when he was on leave—but she hadn't gone out dancing in eleven years. Not since Dad died. Now here she was dancing alone again. She looked happy, but it made me feel sad, for some reason.

Before she noticed I was watching her I went back to the living room.

Matt Parker was fifteen minutes early for dinner. Jenny was still drying her hair and Mom hadn't mixed the onion dip yet.

"I'll be right back," Mom said after she'd greeted him at the door.

"Take your time," he said. I took his brown leather jacket and hung it in the front closet.

"Do you want a—um—something? A—a—beer, maybe?" I stammered. I could feel my cheeks getting warm.

"Could I have a glass of ice water instead?" he asked. I nodded and hurried into the kitchen.

While I was out of the room I heard Aunt Rose come downstairs and introduce herself to Mr. Parker.

"Lisa," Mom said, "just tell them to come in here and sit while I finish fixing dinner."

I swallowed hard.

"Aunt Rose," I said, "Mom says to come into the kitchen and sit."

Aunt Rose smiled at Mr. Parker and they both joined Mom. Mr. Parker pulled out a chair and sat down. He hung his cane over the back. I handed him a glass of ice water.

Pretty soon Jenny came in and started talking to Mr. Parker right away. It was as if she'd known him her whole life. I sat at one end of the table and listened while they talked about Whitney Avenue School, which Mr. Parker had attended a long time ago. Aunt Rose finally got around to Vietnam, and Mr. Parker asked her about the photo essay she was doing.

They talked and talked, and Jenny talked with them as if she were Mr. Parker's oldest friend. I wished I could do that too.

I looked at Mom and wondered if it made her

mad to see her little sister talking so easily to Mr. Parker. Mom hadn't gotten in two words during their entire conversation. Neither had I. The three of them acted like Mom and I weren't even there.

Mom put the dip and chips in front of them, then started ripping up lettuce for the salad.

"Lisa, cut up some more radishes for me, will you?" I nodded, glad to have something else to do.

"This is great dip, Mary Ann," Mr. Parker said. Mom smiled.

At that moment the buzzer on top of the stove went off.

"Dinner's done," Mom said. She grabbed a pot-holder and pulled the broiler pan out of the oven. "Jenny, bring that platter over here."

Jenny brought the blue-and-white plate to the stove. Mom carefully lifted the meat off the pan and slid it onto the platter.

"Lisa, pour water in the glasses while I slice this, will you?"

I reached across Mom to get a pitcher from the cabinet above her.

"Darn," she said. "I think it needs to cook a few more minutes . . ." her voice trailed off.

I looked at the first slice she had cut. The center

looked raw, and bloody juice had oozed onto the plate.

"Oh, yuck," Jenny said. "That's disgusting."

Mom hadn't moved. She was staring straight at the bloody meat. Her face had gone white and her hand shook as she dropped the knife on the counter. Everyone in the room was staring at her. I didn't have to wonder what she was thinking about. It was clear just from looking at her.

"Are you okay, Mom?" I whispered.

"I need some fresh air," Mom said. Her voice quavered. "Lisa, put that . . . that back under the broiler."

Mom opened the back door and went out. She leaned over the porch railing. I prayed she wasn't going to be sick.

"Maybe I'd better go talk to her," I said after I'd put the meat in the oven.

Jenny got up and left the room.

"Why don't you let me?" Matt said. He didn't wait for an answer. He got up from his chair taking his cane with him and walked out to the porch. Through the window in the door I saw him put an arm around Mom's shoulder.

I couldn't hear Mom's voice at all. Every once in

a while I heard Matt's voice, though—not the words, just the sound—soft and soothing. It was helping. When Mom turned around, her cheeks had color in them again.

I watched them while I poured water in the glasses on the table. It was odd how their closeness made me feel. A big part of me was relieved that Matt Parker was there to talk to Mom. But deep down a little part of me was jealous that he knew the right words to say. Words that I would never know.

# Nine

The day of the fall dance, Josh and Heather caught up with me in the hall as I walked to art.

"You're going to be here right when it starts tonight, aren't you?" Heather asked.

"Maybe," I answered. "If I decide to come."

"Hey, you promised," Heather said.

"Yeah, you promised," Josh added. He stuck out his lower lip like a little kid, pouting.

I laughed. "I'll be here," I said.

But I was still worried. What if even Josh didn't ask me to dance?

Josh sat across the room from Heather and me in art class. He kept looking at me over the top of his glasses.

"He's been watching me like that every time we

have art," I whispered to Heather. "What's with him?"

"Besides the obvious—you know he's the kind of person who likes to know what everyone is up to. You're driving him crazy by not telling him what your memorial is going to be about." She giggled and went back to her work. I hadn't told *her* what I was up to either, but she didn't seem to mind. And what was obvious?

I looked over at Josh again. He smiled. I knew it was just a matter of time before his curiosity got the best of him and he came to see what I was working on.

The kids around me were making things out of clay or wood. Others were painting pictures. Heather had designed a wall-hanging with flags and peace signs and she said she was going to write a poem to embroider in the middle.

So far I'd only made a small easel out of wood, and sanded and painted it. That day I also started on a wood frame. Mrs. Smyth helped me mark the angles to make cuts on the table saw. When I was done cutting I glued and stapled the corners together. I was going to do the rest of it at home.

"I knew he couldn't keep his nose out of it," Heather said. "Here he comes." Josh was walking toward our table. He sat on an empty stool beside us.

"O.K. What're you up to?" he asked. I looked right into his eyes and just smiled. I was surprised when his face got red and he coughed like he was embarrassed.

I didn't want to talk about my project yet. Maybe it wouldn't come out like I planned. Maybe I'd have to start over. It was safer if I just talked about it when it was finished.

"Are you going to paint that frame?" he asked.

"I'm not sure what I'm going to do with it," I said. "Can I see what you're working on?" I added before he could ask more.

"Okay." He paused. "Sure. Why not." I knew he wanted to show me his project, but he really wanted to know about mine too.

"Wow" was all I could say when he lifted the cloth from his sculpture. Josh was a much better artist than I had expected. He had made a soldier that looked like a real person. His clothes were wrinkled, his helmet had a dent in it, and his rifle looked like it could really shoot someone. The soldier was sitting on a rock. His hands were on the top of the barrel of the rifle, which was pointed upward. His head was resting facedown on his arms.

"This is good," I said.

"Don't sound so shocked, Lisa. You'll hurt my feelings."

"He looks so real."

"He is," Josh said. "I found a picture like that in a book we have at home. It was perfect for me since I can't do faces. I also liked it because it could be anyone and about anything. This guy could have just seen his best friend killed, or he might be exhausted after a battle, or both. It doesn't matter. Either way—that's what war is about, isn't it?"

I nodded. "Well, it's really good," I said again.

"Thanks." I could tell he was pleased.

I walked to the other side of it. It could have been a sculpture of Dad. It could have been of Matt Parker. Josh was right. That was what was good about it. It could have been almost anyone.

My project wasn't going to look nearly as good as Josh's. But it was too late to come up with anything else now. Besides, even if I could come up with another idea, I still wouldn't be the kind of artist Josh was.

"So, Lisa, are you going to tell me about your memorial?" Josh asked.

"No," I said. Josh's mouth dropped open and I pushed his chin back up to close it. "I'll show you when I'm done. Do you have any ideas for decorating the frame?" I tried to change the subject.

"It's hard to come up with an idea if I don't know what it's about," he said. I stared at him with my lips pressed together. I was not going to tell him.

"You know, Lisa, friends are suppose to tell each other stuff every once in a while."

"I tell you stuff all the time," I said.

"Like what?" he asked.

"Oh, like what we're supposed to do for homework and who Jenny's latest boyfriend is."

"That doesn't count."

"Well, that's the kind of stuff you ask me," I said. "What else do you want to know?"

Josh looked down at the frame I was making.

"Besides that," I said.

"I want to know if you like me," Josh blurted out.

That was the last thing I expected him to say.

"Of course I like you," I said. "You're one of my best friends." I was pretty sure that wasn't what he meant, but I pretended not to understand. How could

I answer a question like that on the spur of the moment? I'd have to practice an answer at least a hundred times at home before I could say the right thing in person. And what *was* the right thing, anyway?

"Oh," he said. Then he walked across the room to his desk.

I looked over at Heather. "I can't believe he asked me that," I whispered.

She bent close to me and whispered back, "He's been in love with you for over a year, stupid."

"He has?"

"Wake up and smell the coffee, Lisa."

"He's one of my best friends," I repeated. That was still true. Wasn't it?

Later in history class Mr. Cooke talked to us about what he was doing during the Vietnam War.

"I did everything to keep from getting sent to Vietnam," he said. "I thought the war was wrong and I didn't want to get killed for something I didn't believe in. I marched in antiwar demonstrations. I had a student deferment for a while. . . ."

"What does that mean?" someone asked.

"It means as long as I was in school I didn't have to go to Vietnam."

"Man, I would have stayed in school until I was a doctor or something," Joe said.

"When I graduated from college I got married. Someone had told me that they wouldn't draft you if you were married."

"Did it work?" Josh asked.

"Well, I didn't get drafted," he said. "But getting married for that reason was a stupid idea and there were days when I thought it would have been better to be in Vietnam." A bunch of boys in the back laughed. I gritted my teeth and sat up in my chair. Mr. Cooke was fighting with his wife while people were getting killed. People like Dad.

"It's not funny," I said. Suddenly everyone was quiet.

Mr. Cooke looked at me, waiting. This time I was going to say what I was thinking and not mess it up.

"No matter how bad your marriage was, it wasn't as bad as what my mom and dad were doing in Vietnam. At least you're still alive."

Mr. Cooke looked down at the floor and then up again, right at me.

"I know," he said softly. "And there are days when that makes me feel very guilty and sad."

He gazed out the window. I saw his neck move as he swallowed.

"Several men—no—boys that I grew up with died there. My friend Al spent thirteen months there. When he came home he was a mess. He cried a lot and got mad a lot. It was hard to still be his friend. Then right before Christmas he seemed happier, calmer . . . better. I thought he was his old self again. Then he shot himself in the head on Christmas Day. I think about him all the time."

I examined the paper I'd been doodling on. I had pressed so hard that it had gone through to my desk. My first thought was how stupid to survive Vietnam and then kill yourself. Mom would never do that. Of course she wouldn't. She couldn't.

I glanced at Mr. Cooke for an instant and then at my notebook. I knew why he'd told us that. He wanted me to know that bad things happened to him too because of Vietnam. But I didn't feel sorry for him.

I stared at him. He cleared his throat.

"I'll always admire the courage of the men and women who served in Vietnam, Lisa. But I'll always believe our government should never have sent them there in the first place. I would protest again if I had it to do all over. I can't change the way I felt—feel—about that, Lisa."

And I couldn't change the fact that Mr. Cooke

was alive and Dad was dead. I knew my own mother had tried to protest the war, but Mr. Cooke still made me mad. I wondered if I would have liked him more if he was missing his legs like Matt Parker. Or if his name was on the Wall like Dad's.

# Ten

I was still mad at Mr. Cooke when Jenny and I walked home that day from school, but after a while I started worrying about the dance instead and forgot to be mad.

"I bet Joe Hansen asks you to dance," Jenny said as we walked along.

"Sure," I said. "And maybe President Reagan will come and lead us all in the bunny hop too."

Jenny laughed. "You're so dumb, Lisa," she said. "I've seen the way Joe Hansen looks at you."

"You're the dumb one," I said. First Josh and now Jenny. What was going on?

"No, I'm not. Lots of boys like you, but you don't even notice. You're so quiet, they think you're not interested."

"So who do you want to dance with?" I asked.

"Oh, I don't know. There's a really cute ninth grader—Ben somebody or other—that I wouldn't mind dancing with, but other than that I don't really care. I won't dance with Brian, though," she said.

Brian was in the seventh grade too. He had been her boyfriend for the last three weeks, but now she hated him. That was the usual for Jenny. No one would ever accuse her of being in the middle of the road about anything.

I let out a long sigh as we trudged up the front steps and inside our house. I wasn't sure at all that someone, anyone, would ask me to dance. After today I didn't think Josh would ever talk to me again.

"This dance stuff really isn't a big deal," Jenny said. She handed me a can of Coke from the fridge. "The boys probably won't ask you on the fast songs anyway. They'll only want to dance to the slow ones and it's easy to dance slow."

"Slow? Slow? Nobody showed me how to dance slow the other night," I practically shouted.

"Stay cool," Jenny said. She put her drink down. "Pretend I'm the boy. Put your arms around my neck, then I put my arms around your waist. Now just try not to step on my toes and I'll try not to step on yours, and we sort of move around the room. See? Easy."

"Easy for you to say," I muttered. I stood dancing with Jenny for a few minutes, looking down at the floor watching our feet. I wondered if Dad would have shown me how to dance if he were here.

Jenny and I danced into the living room, where the phone rang on the end table. Jenny picked it up.

"Hi, Mom," she said. "You're kidding? Mo-om. Please don't, Mom. Pleeeease! Okay, okay. Bye."

Jenny stared at the floor, not saying a word. I wanted to know what was wrong with Mom. It sure changed Jenny's mood in a hurry. With Mom it could be something serious, and I was mad that Jenny was just standing there making me guess.

"So?" I asked.

"Two of the chaperons for the dance are sick with the flu," she said.

"So the dance is canceled?" I asked excitedly.

"Worse," she said. "Mom and Mr. Parker are going to be chaperons."

This was not how I wanted my first dance to go—with my mom watching my every move.

Jenny of course was more dramatic. She buried her head under the sofa cushion and shouted, "My life is over!"

At that moment Aunt Rose came in the door, smiling at us both.

"What's wrong with the princess now?" she asked.

"Mom's going to be a chaperon at tonight's dance," I said.

"I'm ruined!" Jenny whined. She pulled her head out from under the sofa cushion. "Can't you talk her out of it, Aunt Rose?"

"Not a chance," Aunt Rose said. "This is a real step forward for her. It will do her good."

"Mr. Parker is going too," I added.

"Better and better," Aunt Rose said. "Maybe they'll dance."

"Don't even suggest such a horrible thing!" Jenny cried.

"Get hold of yourself, girl. You'll survive," Aunt Rose said. "Take a lesson from your sister. She's not upset. Are you, Lisa?"

I didn't answer. I think I was angry at Mom and angry at myself for being angry. I really wanted some time without Mom around. It didn't seem fair that she would be at my first dance. I was worried enough about other stuff without having to look over at my mom every so often to see if she was all right.

Mom seemed better ever since she'd agreed to talk to my class. Aunt Rose said that preparing for the talk was helping her. But I still worried.

"Mom said she had to work late tonight and she wants to go for a run too," Jenny said. "She'll never be done in time."

"You go get ready," Aunt Rose said. "And I'll make you some grilled cheese sandwiches."

Jenny and I took quick showers, dried our hair, and put on clean jeans and T-shirts. We put on deodorant and spritzed ourselves with Aunt Rose's expensive perfume. Jenny poured us each some mouthwash to gargle with after dinner. She said it was important to smell good all over—which gave me something else to worry about. What if I smelled bad and couldn't tell?

Mom came home and went back out to run while we were eating. Just as we finished dinner, Matt Parker rang the bell.

"I'm early," he said. "But I figured you girls would want to get there right on time."

Jenny gave him a thankful smile. I smiled half-heartedly.

"Come in and sit down," Aunt Rose said. "Mary Ann's gone for a run. She'll be back soon. I'm going to finish cleaning up."

Jenny, Mr. Parker, and I sat in the living room staring at the evening news. When it was over, Jenny got up and put on her coat.

"Let's go," she demanded.

Aunt Rose came into the living room and threw a wet towel at Jenny.

"Hold your horses," she said.

"I'll take them," Mr. Parker said. "Mary Ann can meet us there."

Aunt Rose looked at her watch.

"Okay," she agreed. "I don't know what's keeping her. She said she'd go the short way—wherever that is."

"Yeah, but with Mom that could mean ten miles instead of fifteen," Jenny said.

"Exaggerating again," Aunt Rose teased.

"I've been with her on the short run. It's only three miles," I said.

Aunt Rose looked at her watch again and nodded. She seemed worried. I knew she didn't like

Mom going for runs in the park, especially if it was dark. She was always warning Mom about murderers and rapists and muggers. Mom called her a "worrywart" and said she could outrun them all.

"Let's go, girls," Mr. Parker said.

Aunt Rose stopped looking worried long enough to flash me a thumbs-up sign as we walked out the door.

We could hear the music blaring while we parked the car. It was dark in the gym. The only light came from the hall lights that filtered through the doors, and the red glow of the stereo controls.

Mr. Parker left us right away to talk to Mr. Cooke, who seemed relieved to see him. Jenny went off with her friends and I couldn't see well enough to know if Heather and Josh were there yet or not. I started wishing I was back in my room, or anyplace but standing there by myself.

I felt a hand on my shoulder and turned expecting to see Heather. It was Joe Hansen. My tongue suddenly felt thick and my hands started to sweat.

"Let's dance," he said. Before I could answer he took my hand and led me onto the floor. It was a slow song so I did what Jenny had taught me and put my arms around Joe's neck. He put his arms around my waist. I hoped he couldn't feel how fast my heart was beating. Please don't step on his toes, I prayed to myself.

Joe's warm breath on my cheek smelled like mint and he had on some kind of cologne that smelled musky and sweet. The song finally ended. Joe thanked me for dancing with him and I floated back to the doorway.

I was relieved to see Heather and Josh standing there talking.

"Dancing before we even get here," Heather said. "And with Joe Hansen no less."

Josh didn't look at me. When the next song started, though, he asked me to dance. Heather was asked by the ninth grader that Jenny had had her eye on.

Josh smelled good too—like soap and spearmint gum. He snapped his gum in my ear as we danced and it made me laugh.

"What?" he asked.

"Your gum is pretty loud," I said.

"Sorry," he said. Then he swallowed it. "That will be better."

I laughed again and so did he. I guessed we were

friends again. When the song was over, Josh and I walked back to some chairs set up along the wall.

Jenny waved at me from across the room, and then Josh and I got up to dance for a fast song. Josh danced about like me, but didn't seem at all self-conscious. Nobody else in the room even looked at us. We danced five fast ones together in a row. I was actually starting to like dancing. I hadn't seen Mom, but I figured she must be there someplace.

Finally there was another slow one and I saw Joe Hansen walking toward me. Josh grabbed my hand again and started dancing with me before Joe could say anything. But Joe seemed angry and he kept coming toward us, onto the dance floor. He tapped Josh on the shoulder. I couldn't believe he was trying to cut in. I thought that only happened in the movies. My life was suddenly pretty interesting.

But as usual it didn't last long. Over Josh's shoulder, past Joe, I watched Matt Parker talking on the pay phone. He stood there for a few minutes then put the receiver down and walked over to Mr. Cooke. My stomach did a flip.

"Something's wrong," I said.

"What?" Josh said. I didn't answer, but walked right past Joe and over to Mr. Parker.

"Your mom isn't home yet," he said when he saw me. "Your aunt Rose is worried. I said I'd go look for her. Can you show me where she usually runs?"

I nodded. It figured, I thought angrily. Just when my life was getting exciting Mom had to ruin it. I just wished she'd get well so I could have some fun. I found my sister and told her what was happening.

"Aunt Rose will pick you up when the dance is over if we're not back," I said.

"Leave it to Mom to ruin a perfectly good party," Jenny said.

I felt the same thing. But hearing Jenny say it made me want to defend Mom and made me angry at Jenny—and at myself—for not being more worried about her. Something terrible could have happened to Mom. Maybe Aunt Rose's worst fears had come true.

As I got my jacket a look passed between Mr. Parker and Mr. Cooke. It gave me a hollow feeling and I wished I hadn't seen it.

"Call me as soon as you know something," Mr. Cooke said.

"You got it," Mr. Parker said.

The sound of Mr. Cooke's voice reminded me of the joke he'd made about fighting with his wife during the war and I felt mad at him all over again. Something else he'd said echoed in my mind too. I tried to shut it out. But I couldn't help remembering his friend who'd shot himself on Christmas Day. "He had seemed better . . ." Just like Mom, I thought.

Eleven

Mr. Parker and I stopped by my house for flashlights. Then we went back out into the cold autumn night. Mr. Parker's cane tapped a rhythm on the sidewalk. There was a full moon, which helped some, but it was still awfully dark under the trees.

We walked quickly down the street toward the park without speaking. In the stillness of the night, nagging voices sounded in my head. I heard Aunt Rose warning Mom about running in East Rock Park. I heard Mr. Cooke talking about his friend. I heard Mom screaming for Dad—never mind that she hadn't done that in months.

I told myself I was sure that Mom wouldn't do anything terrible. Mom cared too much about us, didn't she? We needed her and she knew that. At least I hoped she knew that.

At the corner of Livingston and Cold Spring streets we crossed into the park and walked beneath the eerie shadows of the trees. The streetlights barely lit up the path down to the river.

"This is where she starts when she runs along the river," I said. "There are steps first." I didn't want Mr. Parker to fall and then have to worry about him too.

"How far can we go on this path?" he asked.

"It goes to Orange Street. We cross the river up there," I said. "The path starts again a little farther down on the other side."

We walked beside the river, our flashlights reflecting off the water.

"Mom!" I called out.

"Mary Ann!" Mr. Parker shouted.

On the other side of the river we continued calling for Mom every few feet. We heard a snapping and crackling in the brush beside the path and swung our flashlights toward the sound. A fat raccoon lumbered off into the trees.

"There are millions of trails she could have taken," I said. "And I only know a few of them. We're never going to find her."

"Do you think she might have run up to the top—to the lookout?" he asked.

I stood for a minute, thinking. Running to the top of East Rock Park was hard work, especially if you went on the paths instead of the road. Mom was a good enough runner, but she said she was going on a short run.

East Rock was a giant cliff that stood at one side of New Haven. It was sheer rock and could be seen from a long distance away. When we came back from Florida it was my landmark. It was how I knew we were almost home. I'd always liked it before tonight—tonight when Mom might be lost somewhere on it.

My thoughts shifted to the last time I'd been to the top of the rock. I'd gone with Aunt Rose and Jenny. We had walked along the paths and finally up the steep steps built into the face of the rock. At the lookout point you could see all of New Haven and Long Island Sound. I remembered looking over the edge of the cliff and thinking it was a *very* long way down. My head felt dizzy.

"I'll try to find one of the paths," I said. "I think there is one just ahead."

I was lucky and found the four steps that led to the path. We called for Mom and I tried to shut out the voices and the worries that were inside my head. I slipped on a rock and stumbled. Mr. Parker caught my arm and steadied me. I didn't know how someone with two artificial legs and a cane could walk up those paths. I heard his heavy breathing next to me. "Are you okay?" I asked.

"Sure," he said. I didn't believe him.

"Do you want to rest for a minute?"

"No." But we stopped anyway. "The sooner we find your Mom and get out of here, the better I'll feel."

For a moment the moon filtered through the trees. There was sweat streaming down Mr. Parker's face and he looked pale. I put my hand on his arm for a minute.

"I'm okay, Lisa," he said.

I heard Mr. Cooke's voice again in my head.

"How can you stand Mr. Cooke?" I blurted out. "He's such a jerk!"

Mr. Parker laughed. "Your mom told me that you were the calm one in the family," he said. "You've got her fooled, don't you?"

I didn't answer and we continued walking up the hill. Mr. Parker sighed.

"I'd be lying if I said I'd never hated Peter Cooke. But he's a hard person to hate. You know he wrote to me at least once a week when I was in 'Nam?"

"How nice," I muttered.

"Letters from home were the highlight of our week," Mr. Parker went on. "And Peter didn't just write either. He'd send cookies, or books, or the Sunday comics—always something."

"But weren't you mad that he got out of going?" I asked.

"Yeah, I was, at first. I started believing in the war—that's why I volunteered. But Peter thought I was crazy. Said the war was crazy. We had a big fight after I enlisted. But he showed up at the last minute at the bus station to see me off to boot camp. Told me not to be a hero."

"But how could you still be friends when he was back here protesting the war while . . . while . . ."

"While I was getting my legs blown off?" he asked.

"Yeah," I said. And my Dad was getting killed, I thought.

"Well, I didn't want to see him first thing when I came back, that's for sure," he said. Then he chuckled. "But Peter is pretty dense about stuff like that. He was at the hospital even before my mom was there, asking me what I wanted and needed. I was pretty angry and I said I wanted him to get the hell out of there."

I laughed. "Did he go?"

"For a while. But then, he's the one who found me an apartment—on the first floor of a great building. And he's the one who came to visit me all the time. I tried to hate him, but it was hard to when he stayed so loyal no matter how badly I treated him."

"Have you really been friends since you were babies?"

"Yup," Mr. Parker said. "I guess we grew up more like brothers than friends. That's probably why we've stayed close."

I felt a knot form in my throat. My anger for Mr. Cooke had slipped away little by little. I could see why Mr. Parker liked him so much. I cleared my throat.

"Mr. Cooke told us about another friend of his that served in Vietnam," I said. "He survived Vietnam and came home and then . . ." I didn't think I could say it.

"I know," Mr. Parker said. "He was my friend too—for almost as long as Peter had been. I'm the one that found him in his apartment."

I didn't know what to say.

"I think about him every day. When I found him and—and the mess, I promised myself that I would never do that to my family and friends. He gave me the courage to keep living. Some days that's been really hard."

"You mean you've been—you've been—you've had problems too?" I asked.

"Lisa," he said, "when I lost my legs I thought my life was over. But I was lucky. I had friends like Peter—and my family—to cheer me on. I used to drink too much. I used to take drugs. You name it, I tried it. But I'm okay now. Your mom will be too."

I wanted to believe that, but I wondered. If Mom missed Dad enough would she consider suicide?

"Mom!" I called again.

"Mary Ann!"

"Where are you?" I screamed. "Mom!" My voice caught in my throat.

"Lisa," Mr. Parker said. He stopped me on the path. "Take a deep breath."

I did what I was told. I knew why he was doing it, but I wasn't panicking, I insisted to myself. I just wanted to find Mom.

"Before Mr. Cooke mentioned Al, our friend, had you ever thought about it happening to your mom?"

"No," I said. I didn't even have to think about my answer. Before Mr. Cooke's class the thought of Mom killing herself never entered my head. Sure, I'd wondered some nights if Mom might have to go away to a hospital for a while, but I never worried that she'd kill herself. Until now.

"She's always taken care of us," I said. "Aunt Rose helps, but it's mostly Mom who takes care of everything. She's always arranged her work schedule so that she could be with Jenny and me. She never told us about her problems with Vietnam until we were old enough to understand."

I stopped, embarrassed that I was talking so much. When Mr. Parker didn't say anything I kept talking. It made me feel better.

"Aunt Rose said Mom had to tell us so we could understand why she was depressed. And because she needed our support while she worked things out."

"She told me you and Jenny are what keeps her going," Mr. Parker said. "You're very important to her."

The path in front of me looked blurry. I rubbed my eyes.

"Mom!" I yelled. I started to yell again, but Mr. Parker put his hand on my arm and said, "Shhh, listen."

I heard someone calling from far away. I ran up the path, leaving Mr. Parker behind me.

"Mom?"

Then I heard the voice again. It was definitely ahead of me. It sounded like Mom. I ran faster.

"Mom!"

"Here, Lisa," Mom called. I shone my flashlight up the hill where the path curved.

"Mom!" I shouted. I left the path and ran slipping and stumbling over rocks and dried leaves. Mom was sitting on the path with one leg stretched out in front of her. Her ankle looked crooked. I knelt beside her.

"Mom, what happened? Are you okay?" I was shaking all over. Mr. Parker caught up to us. He took his coat off and put it around Mom.

"I went to the top on the road," she said. "Then decided to take a shortcut coming down. Dumb idea. I stepped wrong and fell. My ankle's broken."

Only a broken ankle. I felt tears well up, and my nose started to run. I sniffled.

"Lisa, honey?" Mom said. "I'm going to be okay, really."

"I thought . . . I thought . . ." I couldn't say it.

"Oh, Aunt Rose and her worries," she said. "I

haven't seen a single criminal the whole time I've been here. Only me and a couple of hoot owls."

"Today Mr. Cooke told us about a friend of his who came home from Vietnam and shot himself," I said. I could see understanding fill Mom's face. She put her arms around me.

"Oh, Lisa," she said. "I'd never leave you. I love you and Jenny too much. You know that, don't you?"

I nodded with my head against Mom. I wiped my eyes with my coat sleeve and looked up to see that Mr. Parker was sitting beside Mom on the path. He had his arm around her shoulders.

I looked at Mom's ankle. "Does it hurt a lot?" I asked.

"Yeah," Mom said. "But it will heal."

I smiled at her in the moonlight. Then I looked at Mr. Parker and smiled at him too.

# Twelve

"Boy, you sure go to a lot of trouble to get out of dancing," Josh said on Monday morning.

"Right," I said. I yawned.

"Some people will do anything," Heather agreed.

"Knock it off, you guys." I was still tired from Friday night in the emergency room, and then all weekend running up and down stairs taking Mom food and drinks and doing the laundry. "I had a good time at the dance, really," I added.

"Of course you did," Josh said. "I'm a great dancer. There's another one coming up next month and you owe us."

I remembered my dance with Joe. At that moment he walked by and smiled at me and I thought I might faint.

"How's your Mom?" he asked.

"Fine," I managed to choke out.

He walked off and I saw Josh frowning after him. I was too happy to even care if Josh was mad at me.

"I guess your mom won't be coming to history class today?" Heather asked.

"She has crutches and she says she's coming," I said.

"She's tough," Josh said. "I'd be moaning in my bed eating chips and watching TV if I'd just broken my ankle."

I laughed. "So would I," I said.

It was the last day we had in art class to work on our projects. I knew exactly how mine was going to look now—I had imagined it so many times in my head—and wondered what everyone else, especially Mom, was going to think.

Josh had finished his sculpture last week, and it was already on display in the school lobby. He had nothing else to do so he hovered around where Heather and I were sitting. I was trying to come up with a few lines to explain my project. We were supposed to start with "I wanted to show" or "my project is about," but I couldn't think of more than a one-sentence explanation.

Josh wasn't helping me concentrate either. He fiddled with pencils and tapped on the tables. I knew he was waiting for me to show him what I was doing.

Heather wanted to know too, but she was less obvious about it. She worked with her head bent over the wall-hanging she had made—embroidering one line from a poem. When she thought I wasn't looking she would peer over at me and then at my backpack.

I had planned on finishing my project at home over the weekend. But I was too tired. It would have been easier without Josh and Heather staring at me.

"Did you see Heather's quilt, Josh?" I asked.

"What's it going to say?" he asked.

". . . our best men with thee do go," Heather said.

"That's from a poem by John Donne, isn't it?" he asked.

"How did you know that?" I asked. I didn't think I'd ever get used to the amount of information he seemed to have crammed into his head.

Josh shrugged.

"I was going to write my own poem, but I'm no good at it," Heather said. "Mom gave me a copy of 'Death Be Not Proud.' She read it in college and it always reminded her of the men dying in Vietnam. The poem is way too long to fit on my quilt, but I really liked it. Especially this line."

"What about women?" I asked. "Women served too."

"Ouch!" Heather sucked her stuck finger. I shifted in my seat. I didn't know why I couldn't keep my mouth shut lately. Heather frowned at me. Then she looked down at her work and frowned at it.

"It isn't too late to add 'and women,' " Josh said.

"I can't change a famous poem just like that," Heather snapped.

"Why not?" I asked.

"Why not?" she repeated. Then she said to Josh, "It was less trouble when she was quiet."

She winked at me so I knew she was just teasing. I didn't know if I would be smiling if someone criticized my project.

I pulled out the manila envelope that held the pictures. Josh was standing behind me before I could even open it.

"Mind if I watch?" he asked.

He wasn't self-conscious at all about being so nosy, and it made me laugh.

"Why not?" I said.

"Me too," Heather said. She put her work down and moved her stool closer.

First I pulled out the picture of Mom and Dad and the Vietnamese children and laid it on the table. Aunt Rose had had it blown up into a five-by-seven, which made everything look a little blurry. I thought it looked better that way—like a dream—the two Vietnamese girls standing there holding their Christmas presents with my parents so long ago.

"Is that your dad?" Josh asked.

I nodded.

"Your mom looks pretty even in Army clothes," Heather said. I looked at Mom for a second. While I was always thinking about Mom, I had never thought about her being pretty.

"You're right," I said.

Aunt Rose had also blown up pictures of me and Jenny so that we were the right sizes to match the first picture. I took those pictures out of the envelope and started cutting around our heads—the only part I was going to use.

"Are you making a collage?" Heather asked.

"Sort of," I said. My hands shook as I put Jenny's picture over the head of the girl standing in front of Mom.

"A family collage," Josh said. "Do you want this here?" He put my picture over the older girl. The one standing in front of Dad.

I nodded.

Josh and Heather stared at the picture for a while. Josh handed me a glue stick from his backpack without looking at me. I glued everything together and then wiped my hands on my jeans.

"It's kind of spooky," Heather said at last.

Was it? I tilted my head and looked at it again. I supposed maybe to Heather it was—Dad was dead after all—but in that picture I could see, for the first time, what our family would have looked like.

Josh didn't say anything for a long time. Finally he asked, "Aren't you going to put it in the frame?" He was still looking at my picture. I wondered what he thought of it.

I walked across the room and took the frame and easel down from a metal shelf where I'd left them to dry. I had painted both white. I thought maybe I would decorate the frame with markers. After I put the picture in the frame I set it on the easel.

"Perfect," Heather said. "I bet you get an A."

Josh stared at it.

"Okay," I said. "What's wrong?"

He turned and looked at me. "Nothing's wrong with it," he said. I let out a sigh. "But it isn't perfect. Not yet. It needs a title. You can write it on the frame." He handed me a felt-tipped marker.

"I don't know what to say," I said. I laid the picture flat on the table and removed the cap from the marker.

Heather and Josh stood over me, waiting.

"You guys go away or I'll never think of anything," I said.

Heather sat down and began embroidering again. Josh didn't move.

"Josh, go away," I said.

"I can help," he said.

"Josh, go away," I said again.

He ignored me and picked up the explanation I had been working on.

" 'I wanted to show what my family would have been like if Dad hadn't been killed in Vietnam,' " he read out loud. I tapped the end of the marker against my teeth.

"Maybe you should have said—'I wanted to show

what my family would have been like if Vietnam had never happened'?" Josh said.

"If Vietnam hadn't happened my parents wouldn't have met and I wouldn't be here," I said.

"Oh," he said. He coughed and turned a light shade of pink. I didn't try to make him feel better by telling him I'd almost written exactly that—before I'd thought it through.

"So you made this just for you?" Josh asked changing the subject. "A kind of personal memorial to remember your dad?"

"No," I said without thinking. "I didn't make it for me."

And then I knew what I was going to write. I wrote quickly on the bottom of the frame, "For Mom and Dad."

Josh put his arm around my shoulders.

"Now it's perfect," he said.

I knew he was right.

# Thirteen

"I think your sister wants you," Heather said.

The day had turned warm and we were eating our lunch outside on the grass. I looked where Heather was pointing—near the main classroom building. Jenny was standing there, motioning for me to come over.

"I'll be right back," I said to Heather. I stuffed the sandwich I'd been trying to eat back in the brown paper bag and jogged over to Jenny. I wondered why she hadn't come over to me. Usually she loved talking to my friends.

"I need to talk to you," she said. "I'm worried about Mom."

"She'll be fine. She's been preparing her presentation for weeks." I put my hands on her shoulders.

"She'll be fine," I repeated. I wasn't sure if I was saying that to reassure Jenny or myself.

"But what if this brings on the nightmares again? What if she has a flashback right in the middle of her talk? What if she starts screaming?"

"Mom can handle nightmares and so can we," I said. "And Mom won't start screaming in class."

"But she could."

I stared at my sister. I knew that she was really worried, but having her say all the things I'd been thinking myself just made it worse somehow. And it made me mad.

"You're right," I finally said. "Anything is possible. We could have a major earthquake or a tornado today—and because it hasn't happened before doesn't mean it won't happen now."

Jenny shoved me away from her.

"Why do you always say stuff like that when I get worried?" she said. "I have as much right to worry about Mom as you do."

My throat felt tight.

"Look, Jenny, I'll be in class with Mom in case she has any problems," I said. "Mr. Cooke said you could come if you want."

Jenny shook her head. She didn't look at me.

"Besides, Aunt Rose is going to bring her and stay too," I said.

"Will Matt be there?" Mr. Parker was Matt now—after the night of the broken ankle.

"He has to teach," I said. I didn't tell her that I'd asked him that very morning to come to Mom's talk. He didn't think he could make it. That made me mad. What good was someone who got involved in your family's problems and then wasn't there when you needed him?

The bell rang.

"I gotta go," I said, and ran back to meet Heather.

We met Josh at my locker. I made excuses about having to go to the bathroom and told them to go ahead to history class. I planned to sit in the back of the room. By myself. Near the door. Unfortunately my plan didn't work. Josh and Heather were in the back where they never sit. When I walked in Heather moved her books from the desk next to her.

"Josh told me you'd want to be in the back," she said.

I nodded without really looking at her.

I opened my notebook. My hand shook as I took a pencil from my pencil case and got ready to take notes. I felt pretty stupid—Mom wasn't going to say anything I didn't already know—but holding a pencil somehow made everything seem more normal.

I stared at the chalkboard in the front of the room. Mr. Cooke had written on it "Special Guest Today—Mrs. Grey." I heard Aunt Rose's voice coming down the hall, telling Mom to watch out for that chair and to mind that table. I smiled. Mr. Cooke came in ahead of Mom carrying a box. Our box from the top of the closet with all her Vietnam things in it.

Mom smiled at the class when she entered. She looked pale. I wasn't sure if it was because of the pain in her ankle or because she was scared. When she got to the front of the room she handed her crutches to Aunt Rose. Aunt Rose sat down in the front row and Mom sat on Mr. Cooke's desk with her ankle propped up on top of it. I slid down in my seat and looked at my notebook where I had started drawing spirals in the margins.

Mr. Cooke talked to Mom in low tones for a minute. I couldn't hear what he said, but Mom smiled. I didn't get mad when I looked at Mr. Cooke anymore—not after everything Matt had told me about him. Matt was right. Mr. Cooke was a hard person to hate.

Finally Mr. Cooke introduced Mom—like everyone there didn't already know who she was. Mom reached into the box and pulled out a faded green hat. She put it on.

"I wore this hat when I was in Vietnam," she said. "I haven't worn it since early 1969 when I came home. Today seemed like a good day to put it on again." She gripped the edge of the desk.

"Serving in Vietnam as a nurse for a year was the most difficult thing I have ever done," she said. "In the next hour I hope I'll be able to explain why."

Mom talked on for a while, but I didn't really hear what she was saying. I knew that she was talking about nurse's training and why she joined the Army and about the flight to Vietnam, but it was all just a blur of words.

Josh tapped me on the shoulder and pointed to Mom. She had been talking about uniforms and equipment and now I realized she had been talking to me too.

"I thought you might like to show them your dad's dog tag," she said.

"Um—sure," I said. I pulled the metal tag out from under my shirt. I didn't really want to take the chain off, but I could tell that everyone was waiting for me to pass it around the room. I handed it to Josh first.

"Aren't there usually two tags?" he asked.

"One was buried with my dad," I said, and swallowed hard.

He ran his finger over the back, feeling the bumpy letters pressed into the metal. He read the information on it out loud. " 'Grey. RA'—what does that stand for?" he asked.

"Robert Adam."

"The long number must be the serial number, right?"

I nodded.

" 'M' for male, I guess. Catholic," he said. "Doesn't tell you much about him, does it?" Then he looked at me as he passed the chain to Heather.

"I didn't know you were Catholic," Heather said.

"Dad was," I said.

Mom started talking again when Dad's dog tag got back to me. I didn't put the chain back around my neck. I held the tag in my hand and ran my finger over the familiar letters.

"Some of my worst moments were in the emergency room," Mom said as she took a handful of pictures and started passing them around. I knew that they were pictures of helicopters and empty operating rooms. Mom didn't have time to take pictures when they were full of wounded men.

"These huge Chinook helicopters brought in the wounded. When we had many at one time it was called a mass casualty. The corpsmen would get them from the helicopters and bring them into the hospital.

"The first time we had a mass casualty I couldn't believe how horrible the wounds were. My second day in the hospital I pulled off a soldier's boot and his foot came off with it. I almost passed out.

"Most of the young men were at least four years younger than me—boys, really. It was something I never got used to. But I held together. Those soldiers needed me and I didn't want to let them down."

I had heard most of this before but it still made me want to throw up. I waited for someone to say "yuck" or something, but no one did. The room was silent as Mom went on.

"Once, a wounded soldier was brought in and he begged me to stay with him. He didn't look that bad to me and I needed to see to some of the others. I told him I'd be right back."

Mom closed her eyes for a minute. I knew what she was going to say. I squeezed Dad's dog tag harder.

"When I got back to him he was dead. I couldn't believe it. I turned him over and found a gaping hole in his back. I felt awful that I hadn't been with him. I felt like I had killed him. I never left anyone alone again who asked me to stay, if I could help it."

Mom took a deep breath and so did I.

"I only remember the name of one of the boys who came through our hospital in Vietnam," she said. "He gave me his picture right before he died. He said it was so I wouldn't forget him. I never have."

Mom took out the picture of Scott Boyd and passed it around. She told them the story she had told me and Jenny. About how he'd been wounded three times and each time she'd taken care of him. How she stayed up with him all night holding his hand and writing letters to his mom and girlfriend.

Mom stared out the window for a moment while everyone silently handed Scott's picture around the room. She went on.

"In Vietnam the doctors taught the nurses procedures that only doctors performed in a regular hospital. It saved time—lives. It was very hard to return to a U.S. hospital and not be allowed to do the things I had learned. I wasn't given as much responsibility here. That was one of the things I missed about Vietnam."

I sat up in my seat. She'd never said that she missed anything about Vietnam before.

"I said at the beginning that serving in Vietnam was one of the most difficult years of my life. It was more than that. It was one of the worst years of my life." That was more like it.

Mom looked right at me. I wanted to tell her she was doing great, that I was proud of her, but I couldn't right there in front of everyone so I just smiled. She smiled back.

"Vietnam was also one of the best years of my life," Mom went on. I stopped smiling and my mouth dropped open. I closed it quickly.

Mom held up the big picture of Dad that was normally beside her bed.

"I met Lisa and Jenny's father there," she said. "We didn't have long together, but I wouldn't have missed it for the world."

Okay, I knew that. But surely that was the only good thing.

Mom took out another stack of pictures. She held one up of her standing with one arm around a man and her other arm around a woman.

"The friends I made there and the closeness I felt with the people I worked with during the war is like no closeness I've ever felt again—except with the members of my family. In wartime the people you work with become your family.

"We were always busy at this hospital. Always. But we still found time to have a party every once in a while, or just sit and talk."

Slowly the pictures she had pulled out of the box drifted back to Heather and Josh and me. They were pictures I had seen before. But for the first time I was noticing the smiles. Most of the people looked like—right at that moment when the camera snapped their images—they were happy. Parties held in bunkers made out of sandbags. Mom holding a beer, sitting on someone's lap. A group of soldiers playing volleyball.

Then Mom showed us a picture of a nurse holding a baby. I didn't recognize it.

"I found this picture tucked away in a drawer the other night. It reminded me of another good thing that happened in Vietnam. I got to deliver a baby." Mom smiled.

"A very pregnant Vietnamese woman walked in. She was in a lot of pain. There was no one else around so I put her on a cot. Before I could call a doctor the woman pushed and strained and in a few minutes I was holding a new baby boy in my arms." A couple of kids giggled. "It was such a wonderful sight to see new life in the middle of all that death."

Mom looked down at the floor for a minute, then leaned forward, stretching her back. Then she looked toward the doorway and smiled. I turned and saw Matt Parker. I wondered how long he'd been standing there. He smiled too.

Mom didn't look so pale anymore. I didn't think it was just because Matt was there either.

"I want to thank you for asking me to come and talk to you. Preparing this helped me start remembering some of the good things that happened to me in Vietnam," she said.

I listened without hearing to the questions the kids in my class asked Mom. Slowly the knots in my stomach started to ease. I stared out the window at the golden leaves drifting to the ground. The clapping that signaled Mom was done jolted me out of my daydream.

Mom was saying thank you again and Aunt Rose was helping her get her crutches under her arms.

"Next week I'll be going to the dedication of the

Vietnam Veterans Memorial with Mrs. Grey, her family, and Mr. Parker," Mr. Cooke said. I knew that Matt was going but I hadn't known about Mr. Cooke. "When we come back Mrs. Grey's sister will share her photographs of the Wall with our class."

Aunt Rose waved as she helped Mom out the door. I slipped Dad's dog tag over my head. I didn't bother to put it under my shirt now.

"You're so lucky," Heather whispered.

"Why?" I asked.

"You get to see the Wall," she said.

Somehow *lucky* didn't seem quite the right word.

# Fourteen

"Sorry about this." The cabdriver turned to smile at us. Jenny, Matt, Mom, and I were squashed together in the back seat of his taxi with Mom's crutches lying across our laps. Mr. Cooke and Aunt Rose were sitting up front. Aunt Rose was already snapping pictures out the window.

On the map the train station hadn't looked that far from the memorial, but it was taking forever. We were stopped in the middle of the street surrounded by hundreds of cars all going in the same direction.

"Normally this would be a ten-minute cab ride—fifteen, tops," he went on. "But not today."

I looked nervously at the clock on the dashboard—one-thirty. The dedication ceremony was going to start at two o'clock and I didn't want to miss it. Somebody had to be there for Dad.

"We'll make it by two, won't we?" I asked.

"I'll do my best," the driver said. Then he shook his head. "It's been like this all week. Who would have believed that so many would come here to honor Vietnam vets? It's about time."

"You a vet?" Aunt Rose asked. She snapped his picture.

"No. Too young," the man said. He looked at Mr. Cooke. "You look like the right age."

Mr. Cooke cleared his throat and shook his head.

"Matt and Mary Ann were in Vietnam," he said, pointing to the back seat. "Mary Ann's husband was killed there."

The driver whistled.

"No wonder you want to be in time for the ceremony," he said. He leaned on his horn. "This is important."

The traffic began to creep forward.

"Maybe we should walk," Mom said. "It isn't much farther, is it?"

"No, ma'am," the driver said. "But to tell you the truth, with so many people on the sidewalks,

I think you'd have trouble getting through with your crutches."

I let out a sigh and leaned back against the seat. What if we missed the ceremony after all this rushing—and worrying? We just couldn't.

If I had to, I decided, I would get out and run ahead of everyone. Mr. Cooke had already given each of us the name and address of the hotel we would stay in that night and a map in case we got separated. He said it was hard to quit acting like a teacher trying to keep track of his students on a field trip.

The cabdriver honked the horn again. Other cars around us echoed the sound. We moved a few more inches then stopped again.

"Sorry," Jenny whispered to me.

"It's okay," I whispered back. She was the reason we'd missed an earlier train out of New Haven. That train would have arrived in Washington, D.C., by noon, and we would have had two hours to get to the memorial. But Jenny had been in the bathroom throwing up her breakfast, so we couldn't leave. Mom thought she might be coming down with something. I thought it was just worrying.

I moved my backpack off my legs and onto my

feet on the floor. It held the homework I planned to do Sunday night on the train home, plus a change of clothes and a toothbrush. And it held my art project—my memorial. Mrs. Smyth had given it back to me on Friday just before school let out. She gave me an A on it and asked if she could put it up in the lobby next to Josh's sculpture. I said no. I wanted to show Mom first.

But then that night with everyone excited about the trip and rushing around getting laundry done and dinner fixed—I somehow never had the chance to show it to her. Maybe I hadn't wanted to. I didn't know why. Maybe I was afraid she wouldn't like it. Or afraid that she'd get too upset right before the trip. Or maybe I just wanted to keep it to myself for a while.

"Come on, you guys!" The cabdriver stuck his head out the window and shouted. "Get a move on!"

We inched forward. The minutes ticked by.

"We're pretty close now," the driver said. "I don't think I can get you much closer by two."

Everyone started to get out and Matt reached for his wallet from his back pocket.

"You keep your money where it is," the driver said. "I'm not taking money from vets or their families

today. That's my way of saying thanks." He smiled
and jumped out to open the door for us. He helped
Mom to the sidewalk and handed her the crutches.

"It's that way," he said. "I think you can just make it."

"Thanks," Mom said. Aunt Rose stood beside
her taking pictures as fast as she could. I wasn't even
sure what she was taking shots of.

Matt and Mr. Cooke shook the driver's hand. He
waved.

I shivered even before the cold wind blew my
jacket open and chilled the chain that held Dad's
dog tag. We made our way through the masses of
people. There seemed to be thousands. Could it be
possible that all these people knew someone whose
name was written on the Wall?

Everywhere I looked I saw men and women in
uniforms. Like the ones Mom and Matt wore in
their pictures. Medals covered some. People held
signs and wore T-shirts that said things like "Never
forget" and "No more wars. No more lies." One
sign even said "I need a job." There were people in
wheelchairs and on crutches. People were laughing
and talking, crying and hugging on their way to the
Wall. Aunt Rose took pictures of it all.

Mom took the hat she'd worn in front of our

class out of her backpack and put it on. Matt was already wearing one. And pinned to his leather jacket were his medals—a Purple Heart for being wounded and two bronze stars for heroism. Dad also had a Purple Heart and two stars, except one of his stars was silver for gallantry in battle.

I hated that definition. It sounded too much like the words to a fairy tale where the brave knight lived happily ever after. Dad was awarded the silver star because he gave his life trying to save his buddies. Jenny was wearing Dad's medals pinned to her T-shirt under her coat. I pulled Dad's dog tag and held it tight with one hand.

As we got closer we could hear a man's voice over a loudspeaker talking about God and eternal peace. I realized he was saying a prayer only when he said amen. I repeated amen without thinking. We kept walking forward until we couldn't get any closer. There were people packed in all around us. Children were sitting on their fathers' shoulders and people were sitting in trees, trying to get a better look.

"This isn't fair," Jenny said. "We're finally here and I can't even see Dad's memorial. I'm too short."

I put my arm around her shoulders.

"We'll stay here all night if we have to to get a good look at Dad's name," I said. "Don't worry."

"Here, sweetheart," a man said. He plunked down at Jenny's feet a plastic milk crate he'd been standing on. "You and your sister can stand on this."

Before we could say thanks the man in his faded green clothes had stepped into the crowd and drifted away.

Jenny and I stood on the milk crate together. Mom, Matt, Mr. Cooke, and Aunt Rose stood in front of us so we could balance holding on to their shoulders. Ahead, down a little slope, was a dark black V-shaped wall. It looked like the pictures Mrs. Smyth had shown in art class. It was low at each end and gradually got higher until it reached the tallest point in the middle.

In the pictures I had seen, the Wall didn't appear to be so big. But even from where we stood I could see that it was incredibly long and almost twice as tall in the center as the people standing near it. I couldn't see the 58,000 names, but I knew they were there. Waiting.

The speeches took forever. The people around me seemed interested in what was being said, but I barely heard anything except for occasional words and the hum of the tenors and basses of the voices that said them. I felt queasy and light-headed, and wondered if I was catching what Jenny had.

Finally everyone was singing "God Bless America." Jenny and I sang along.

Then a man said, "The Vietnam Veterans Memorial is now dedicated."

All around us people cheered. Jenny and I found ourselves pushed off the crate and moved along toward the Wall with the mass of people.

"Stick close," Mom said over her shoulder. Her face looked almost as gray as the dreary sky above. Matt walked beside her, stumbling every so often. It was as if his plastic legs were suddenly too heavy for him. He carried three cans of beer in a paper sack. I was pretty sure I knew why. Mr. Cooke took Jenny's and my hands and followed close behind them.

I held tight to Dad's dog tag with my free hand. If the chain broke it would be lost forever. I wasn't taking any chances.

"We'll never get to the Wall," Jenny said. Mom didn't seem to hear her. She just kept moving through the crowd. Closer to the Wall. Aunt Rose leaned over and gave Jenny a hug.

A man climbed on top of the Wall and put a

bugle to his mouth. Slowly and clearly he played taps, which I'd heard before in old war movies. Mom had told me it was often played at military funerals. It sounded sad and made my throat feel tight. Aunt Rose took his picture.

After what seemed like hours we were still a few feet from the center of the Wall. It towered over our heads, making me feel small. The surface of the Wall was shiny and reflected the faces of the crowd. From a distance the reflections weren't clear. They looked like ghosts.

"We don't even know where to look," Mom said.

"Ask her," Jenny said, pointing to a woman in a yellow hat. People were surrounding her, asking questions. With Aunt Rose's help Mom moved toward the guide, saying "excuse me" every few seconds as if she was a robot programmed to move ahead no matter what. Mr. Cooke, Jenny, and I followed. Matt walked away from us toward a man in a yellow hat. He had his own questions to ask.

We waited our turn to talk to the woman. When at last she looked at my mother with raised eyebrows, Mom seemed startled.

"My husband," she stammered.

"What was his name, ma'am?" the guide asked softly.

"Grey," Mom said. "Robert Adam."

The woman turned pages in a big book full of names and ran her finger down the list. My chest felt tight. Had there been a mistake? Had they forgotten to put Dad's name on the wall?

"How do you spell Grey?" the woman asked. "With an *a* or an *e*?"

"*E*," Aunt Rose said before Mom could answer.

The guide nodded and turned a page.

"Here we are," she said. "Panel four west. Line one-twenty. This way."

I let out the breath I had been holding and took in great gulps of cold air.

We followed her as she helped Mom move through the maze of people. I squeezed Dad's dog tag with one hand and held Jenny's hand with the other. My heart was pounding in my ears. What was Mom thinking? Did she want to run away? A part of me wanted to.

Around us I watched as people reached to touch the Wall. Others leaned over the edge of the Wall from above. Everyone wanted to touch the name of someone they loved.

One woman held her grown son's hand up to a name just within reach.

"Your father," she said. Her son bent his head

toward hers and they seemed to be saying a prayer together. Then they hugged each other as if they never wanted to let go.

Three men stood close together and each put a hand on the same name. They all closed their eyes, but their tears leaked out anyway.

"Look," Jenny said. "People are making rubbings of the names. Can we do that?"

I nodded, thankful to be carrying paper and pencils.

"Here," the guide finally said. She left us standing there counting the lines down from the top. Dad's panel was four from the center and really tall. It made me feel as if I was buried in names.

I was still looking for Dad's name when I heard Mom say "here," echoing what the woman in the yellow hat had said. Mom knelt in front of the Wall. Aunt Rose held her crutches. She had stopped taking pictures. Mom had her hand on a name just in front of her. Jenny and I knelt beside her. When she moved her hand I could read Dad's name— Robert Adam Grey.

Jenny and I reached out to touch Dad's name too. It was warm and solid. I felt wetness on my cheeks and a knot in my throat that I knew could only be cried away. Mom covered our hands with her own as tears slipped down her cheeks. She put her arms around us finally and pulled us close to her. Aunt Rose reached out to touch Dad's name too.

"I miss him so much," Mom said.

"I know," Aunt Rose said. She put her hand on Mom's shoulder.

"I wish we could have known him," Jenny said.

I did too, but I couldn't speak.

"I wish," Mom said, looking up toward the top of the Wall and the sky, "that I could have done more for all these men. That I could have saved more of them." And then she whispered, "I should have tried harder."

A stranger's hand patted Mom on the shoulder. She was kneeling next to Mom.

"We've all thought that. But you have to believe that you did your best," she said. "That's all anyone could expect of you. Of any of us." The woman had on a hat like Mom's. She and Mom hugged for a moment.

I wanted to hug this woman I'd never seen before. She had been a nurse in Vietnam too. I wondered how many nurses had flashbacks and nightmares like Mom. Did they have children who worried about them and wondered if they would be okay? I knew that some of them must. Thousands of families just like ours had been changed forever by Vietnam.

I took paper and pencil from my backpack and handed them to Jenny. I looked up and down the length of the Wall while we waited for her to make rubbings. People had left things all along the Wall.

Flowers, of course, but other things too. There were letters and medals, dog tags and books. A few panels away Matt sat down on the ground. He took the three cans of beer out of his paper sack and lined them neatly in a row in front of him. He was finally buying the beer for his buddies that he'd promised them.

Mr. Cooke took a photo of a stern-looking young man in a uniform out of his pocket. He pinned a bronze star to the picture. Then he took out a pen and wrote the name Alexander Thompson in the white area around the photograph. I watched as he placed the picture at the foot of the panel next to Dad's. He was crying. He saw me watching when he turned around.

"His name should be here too," he said. I knew

that this was a picture of his friend who had shot himself. I hugged Mr. Cooke then. It seemed like the right thing to do.

"We should have brought something to leave," Mom said.

At the base of Dad's panel was a picture. A big one of a mother and her three children. Across the bottom was written "Sam, look how well they've turned out! I'll always love you, Amy."

I slowly unzipped my backpack again. I pulled my art project from it and handed it to Mom without looking at it.

"We could leave this," I said. Mom gasped as she took it. I rushed on. "I made it in art class. I was going to show it to you last night . . . I have copies of it at home . . ."

Mom pulled me close to her.

"It's beautiful," she said. She placed it on the ground in front of the Wall.

Then Mom, Jenny, and I knelt there with our arms around each other for a long time—staring at our reflection in Dad's name.